# Harmattan

Insurrections: Critical Studies in Religion, Politics, and Culture

SLAVOJ ŽIŽEK, CLAYTON CROCKETT, CRESTON DAVIS,
JEFFREY W. ROBBINS, EDITORS

The intersection of religion, politics, and culture is one of the most discussed areas in theory today. It also has the deepest and most wide-ranging impact on the world. Insurrections: Critical Studies in Religion, Politics, and Culture will bring the tools of philosophy and critical theory to the political implications of the religious turn. The series will address a range of religious traditions and political viewpoints in the United States, Europe, and other parts of the world. Without advocating any specific religious or theological stance, the series aims nonetheless to be faithful to the radical emancipatory potential of religion.

For a list of titles in this series, see page 175.

# Harmattan

A PHILOSOPHICAL FICTION

MICHAEL JACKSON

Columbia University Press
New York

Columbia University Press
*Publishers Since 1893*
New York    Chichester, West Sussex
cup.columbia.edu
Copyright © 2015 Columbia University Press
All rights reserved

Library of Congress Cataloging-in-Publication Data

Jackson, Michael, 1940– author.
Harmattan : a philosophical fiction / Michael Jackson.
pages cm. — (Insurrections)
ISBN 978-0-231-17234-9 (cloth)—ISBN 978-0-231-17235-6 (paperback)—
ISBN 978-0-231-53905-0 (e-book)
1. Kuranko (African people—Social life and customs.    2. Kuranko (African
people)—Folklore.    3. Ethnology—Sierra Leone.    4. Jackson, Michael,
1940– —Travel—Sierra Leone.    5. Philosophical anthropology.
I. Title.    II. Series: Insurrections.

DT516.45.K85J29 2015
128—dc23
2014034074

Cover design: Catherine Casalino
Cover image: © 2012 Debora Moraes/Getty

I've created various personalities within. I constantly create personalities. Each of my dreams, as soon as I start dreaming it, is immediately incarnated in another person, who is then dreaming it, and not I.

To create, I've destroyed myself. I've so externalized myself on the inside that I don't exist there except externally. I'm the empty stage where various actors act out various plays.

— Fernando Pessoa, *The Book of Disquiet*

# Contents

## 1 Limitrophes    1

Show and Tell    1

A Place in the Bush    3

Allegories of the Wilderness    3

Within and Without Limits    5

The Top Five Regrets of the Dying    10

Life Is Elsewhere    12

Dark Soundings    16

On Not Being Rule Governed    20

Confronting One's Demons    23

Renata    26

Sentiments Limitrophes    30

The Faraway Tree    31

What Lies Beneath    35

Schrödinger's Cat    36

Notes    39

## 2 Harmattan    45

Stories Happen    45

*Thousands Bay*    46

*Persona Non Grata*    47

*Tom Lannon's Story*    55

*Cosmega*    64

*Sangbamba*    75

*Ezekiel's Story*    94

*Petra's Letter*    111

*No Condition Is Permanent*    124

*The School*    134

*Morowa*    136

*Night*    151

*After Fieldwork*    166

*Mistral*    171

# Harmattan

# Part One

# Limitrophes

Limitrophe: situated on a border or frontier; bordering on, adjacent to. French, from Late Latin *limitrophus*, bordering upon, literally, providing subsistence for frontier troops, irregular from Latin *limit-*, *limes* boundary + Greek *trophos* feeder, from *trephein* to nourish.

—*Merriam-Webster Dictionary*

## Show and Tell

For many years I was convinced that a clear line should be drawn between documentation and invention, particularly in ethnographic writing, where one's first obligation is to do justice to the experience of those who welcomed or tolerated one's presence in their communities. It is all very well borrowing narrative conventions, figurative language, and montage from fiction, poetry, and cinema in order to give life to a text and counteract the deadening effects of academic jargon and abstraction—something I had done in several ethnographic books written for a general rather than specifically academic readership.[1] But such experimentation, I believed, should avoid blurring the distinction between fiction, which freely invents other worlds and other lives, and ethnography, whose focus is on actual events, experiences, and persons. Nevertheless, as a poet, fiction writer, and ethnographer, I have always been drawn to such classics of philosophical fiction as Jean-Paul Sartre's *La Nauseé*, Albert Camus' *L'Etranger*, Kurt Vonnegut's *Slaughterhouse Five*, Herman Melville's *Moby-Dick*, and Joseph Conrad's *Heart of Darkness*. Attracted to the idea of *juxtaposing* showing and telling, I share Derrida's dream of a writing that would be neither philosophy nor literature, but keep alive a memory of both.[2] Might it not be more reader friendly and illuminating to interleave the distilled and generalized knowledge so characteristic of the academy with the more aporetic, eventful, and nondiscursive forms of literature? Against the European philosophical tradition that has sought to keep these modes of writing separate (assuming being and thought to be nonidentical), I draw my inspiration from a Kuranko perspective in which there is a *complementary* relationship between foundation myths (*kuma kore*, lit. "venerable speech") that are held to be "true," and antinomian tales (*tilei*) that are admittedly make-believe. While myths support the status quo—the authority of chiefs, the wisdom of elders, the alleged inferiority of women, the importance of tradition—folktales play with reality, challenging hierarchy, reversing roles, and exploring fantastic possibilities for righting wrongs and redressing injustices.

Because it does not follow that what is necessary for the common weal is equally imperative for every individual, there is in Kuranko society—as in human societies everywhere—an ironic counterpoint between the discursive values articulated in myth and the subversive tactics deployed in folktales. To cite Derrida, every culture bears traces of an alterity that refuses to be domesticated; every culture is haunted by its other.[3] While myths lay down the law, reinforce respect for received values, and draw attention to the ancestral or divine underpinnings of the social order, fictional narratives address quotidian problems of injustice, reveal the frailty of authority, mock the foibles of men, and shame all those who mask their greed and ambition with the language of ideology and the trappings of high office.

This indeterminate relation between knowledge and life also informs the structure of this book. While grounded in empirical research and real events, I increasingly depart from reality in order to *show* what could not otherwise be told.

## A Place in the Bush

Northeast Sierra Leone. December 1969. In a few days it will be Christmas, but as Noah Marah and I cross the Seli River and begin our trek to Firawa, Christmas is far from our thoughts. Our path has been trodden by generations of bare or sandaled feet. The air is filled with filigrees of burned elephant grass that settle on the path like colons and commas, punctuating our way. Occasionally the conical thatched roofs of a farm hamlet appear above the tawny grassland, and we meet men and women toting bundles of firewood or sacks of rice on their heads. They exchange greetings with Noah, while peering at me from beneath their head loads. When Noah is asked who I am, he tells them I am an old pen friend who has come to visit his natal village. As for me, I am in a state of trance, as if passing from one incarnation into another. A succession of grass-covered plateaus drifts into the bluish haze of the Loma Mountains. Saurian rock formations, such as I had never seen before, rise out the landscape, yet appear to recede as we approach them. Noah says that when a man from a ruling lineage is about to die, you may hear snatches of xylophone music borne on the wind and the creaking of granite doors as the djinn who inhabit the inselberg prepare to receive another soul into their midst.

## Allegories of the Wilderness

On my second night in Firawa, a group of men, women, and children gather on the porch of Noah's brother's house to tell stories. As Noah summarizes each story for me, I am struck by recurring scenarios and motifs. A marginalized or maligned individual—an orphan, an oppressed junior wife, a status inferior—journeys into the bush where he or she is cared for by djinn. Empowered and enriched, the erstwhile victim returns to the village that spurned him or her and receives the recognition or blessings that he or she is due.

The djinn may therefore be compared with the figure of the daemon in European thought: a redistributor of human destinies.

As the days pass into weeks, I begin to understand the ramifications of the contrast between village and bush in Kuranko discourse. The bush is construed as a wild but fecund force field surrounding the settled space of a village. This is not only because rice—the staple of life—is cultivated in farm clearings slashed and burned in the bush, or because medicinal plants are gathered, and game animals hunted, in the bush; movements between town and bush are allegories of life itself and call to mind the classical Greek antinomy of *nomos* (law) and *phusis* (life). While community coexistence depends on binding legal and moral laws, personal fulfillment in life depends on more than slavish conformity to established norms, dutiful role-playing, or adherence to tradition. It involves going beyond the social world into which one is born and tapping into life itself, which knows no bounds.

Almost all Kuranko tales involve journeys between town (*sué*) and bush (*fira*). As such, the moral customs (*namui* or *bimba kan*), laws (*seriye* or *ton*), and chiefly power (*mansaye*) associated with the town are momentarily placed in abeyance, and the wild ethos of the bush, associated with animals, shape-shifters, djinn, and antinomian possibilities, comes into play. Moreover, Kuranko stories are told at night, or in twilight zones that lie on the margins of the workaday, waking world. There is a close connection, therefore, between the evocation of antinomian scenarios, states of dreamlike or drowsy consciousness, and the narrative suspension of disbelief. Kuranko *tilei* (fables, folktales, fictions) are make-believe; they play with reality, and entertain possibilities that lie beyond convention and custom.

But do people everywhere feel compelled to come into their own by moving beyond the world into which they were born, breaking with the settled routines and habitual patterns that they were raised to regard as second nature? And is it always the case that when we are stretched to the limit we experience life with such ecstatic sharpness and painful clarity that we will declare these moments to be more existentially nourishing, and more real, than anything we find within our comfort zones and everyday routines? Does the road of excess always lead to the palace of wisdom?

In Firawa I began to realize that whatever knowledge I might wrest or distill from my sojourn there was less important than the change that might be wreaked in myself by allowing this remote lifeworld to work on my imagination and revolutionize my thinking. In construing the ethnographic project in this way, I was already outside the academic pale, though few would argue against the view that ethnography is an essay in understanding one's humanity from the standpoint of what at first sight appears to be incomprehensible and alien, venturing beyond the margins of one's own familiar world to explore the human condition from a radically different point of view.

## Within and Without Limits

Life on earth is vaster and more various than the lifeworlds of human beings. Yet we live, alone or together, in symbiotic relationships with the myriad, multifarious, and microscopic forms of life that inhabit the forests, grasslands, deserts, waterways and seas that surround us. While we may be unique in possessing a *conceptual* life, our existence depends on the plants and animals we eat, the timber we use for building, the bacteria, fungi and viruses in and on our bodies,[4] and the companion creatures to which we become attached. This extrahuman life not only nourishes our bodies and souls; it is the source of the metaphors with which we think, the gifts we give, and the imagery of art and religion. Although it is not uncommon for intellectuals to declare that we have reached a point in our evolution when the line between nature and culture has been blurred or abolished, with virtual and built environments displacing the "natural" environments in which our ancestors struggled to survive, the interplay between human lives and life itself remains existentially fundamental. This is nowhere more dramatically evident than in tribal societies where being is not limited to human being but distributed beyond the world of living persons—a potentiality of ancestors, divinities, (totemic) animals, objects (fetishes), and even plants.

In this view it would be a mistake to regard any one particular life form, such as our own species, as higher or more privileged than others.

In this book I explore our relationship with life itself through the image of the limitrophe.

The word *limitrophe* derives from the Latin *limes* ("boundary") and the Greek *trophos* ("feeder") and *trephein* ("to nourish"). In its original meaning, *limitrophus* designated lands that provided food for troops defending an outpost of empire. More generally, the word denotes a borderland between two or more states, though it also calls to mind Gloria Anzaldúa's notion of a *mestiza* consciousness where "phenomena collide"[5]—a destabilized and transgressive borderlands in which "dreams, repressed memories, psychological transferences and associations" possess greater presence than they do in ordinary waking life and religious experiences emerge from the unconscious like apparitions.[6] Mention might also be made of Frederick Jackson Turner's frontier thesis that the American spirit of democracy was nourished by "the American forest, and . . . gained new strength each time it touched a new frontier."[7] The frontier fostered independence and simplicity and provided a clean break with old world pretensions and arcane mannerisms. There are echoes, too, of being Beyond the Pale, a phrase that dates back to the fourteenth century, when the part of Ireland that was under English rule was bounded by a line of stakes or fences, known as the English Pale. To travel outside that boundary, beyond the pale, was to leave behind all the rules and institutions of English society, which the English considered synonymous with civilization itself.

I adapt the term *limitrophe* to describe, ethnographically and autobiographically, the life-giving potential of places, people, and powers that lie beyond the pale of our established lifeworlds and to show that existential vitality depends on going beyond what has been prescribed by custom, internalized as habit, or enshrined in received ideas of truth and reality.

This theme has preoccupied me from the time I did my first fieldwork among the Kuranko and found myself mystified as to why people devoted so much time to ritually, playfully, narratively, and politically *dis*organizing or *dis*membering their lifeworlds only to produce situations that closely resembled the ones they overthrew.[8] It wasn't as if people were working to overthrow the social order; rather that they needed to determine that order for themselves and not feel that *it* determined them. In this way they connived in the creation of their own worlds, even as they worked to create a world they shared with others. I discerned this phenomenon in Kuranko initiation ritual, storytelling, and everyday palaver when people playfully picked quarrels with each other, made mountains out of molehills, or prolonged a court case with seemingly needless digressions while I stood by, wondering why instrumental reason appeared less imperative than the need to have one's say or make one's presence felt. There were times when I felt I was seeing the world through Lewis Carroll's looking glass. Human beings resembled Humpty Dumpty. Although you are a perfectly intact egg, sitting well balanced on a wall, you nevertheless pick yourself up periodically and dash yourself to pieces, only to put yourself back together again. The process may be seen in both individual and collective life.

How can it be explained?

Life may be full of contingency and unpredictability, and you may feel powerless in the face of forces outside your comprehension and control, but in these seemingly trivial and perverse actions of disintegration and reintegration you preempt what you fear may befall you, acting as if the world were yours to unmake and remake on your own terms, in your own time. For a moment you are no longer a bit player in someone else's drama, or an extra under someone else's direction; you take center stage, you call the shots.

Though I regard it as axiomatic that human beings strive to experience themselves as free in some small measure to make, unmake and remake the world into which they are thrown by circumstances beyond their control, they readily shy away from such dramatic transformations *when these are imposed upon them against their will*. Just as soldiers quail at the thought of being sent to a war-torn frontier, we all suffer the qualms and anxieties that attend the passage from the known to the unknown. When working in an Aboriginal settlement in Central Australia, I would hear rumors of small boys running away from initiation, fearful of the ordeals that awaited them in "business camp." In southeast Sierra Leone, neophytes live in dread of the crocodile that will allegedly swallow and regurgitate them. In families across the world, adolescents suffer that sinking feeling in the pit of their stomachs as they prepare to leave home for college in a distant city. Sometimes we have to be coerced or tricked into undertaking these initiatory journeys. Often we will take the plunge because of peer pressure or simply to save face. Though our fulfillment in life may depend on braving the perils of the unknown, our faintheartedness is a reminder of our need to be secure in the lives we know, as well as strong enough to risk ourselves in the wilderness of the wider world. And, even if we don't take risks ourselves, we often identify with those that do, vicariously casting ourselves away on a desert island, walking on hot coals, climbing Everest, exploring the Amazon, walking on the moon.

At the end of his account of a traumatic near-death experience in the Peruvian Andes (*Touching the Void*), Joe Simpson asks what his life would have been like had he not faced death on Siula Grande.

> A part of me thinks that I would have gone on to climb harder and harder routes taking greater risks each time. Given the toll of friends over the years I'm not confident I would be alive today. In those days I was a penniless, narrow-minded, anarchic, abrasive and ambitious mountaineer. The accident opened up a whole new world for me. Without it I would never have discovered hidden talents for writing and public speaking . . .
>
> In Peru we had gone to unusual lengths to take the ultimate risk and yet despite all the pain and trauma it now seems a small price to pay for such an inspiring adventure. Isn't memory a wonderful deceiver? Almost losing everything in Peru was a sensation quite as life-enhancing as winning.[9]

Such yearnings for excess, darkness, altered states of consciousness, and the extramundane are often associated with youth, not old age. Children typically test the boundaries of what their parents decide and define for them. In this way, they experiment with their individual capacities to define the world for themselves. When my daughter Freya was eighteen months old, she was given a toy pram that she wheeled through the park and around the house, brooking no interference from her parents, jealous of her autonomy, and exhilarated by her mastery of a situation she had hitherto lived in passivity—being wheeled around in her pram by others. Six months later, Freya's self-assertiveness was even more noticeable. "No, me do it, Daddy," was her continual refrain, except at bedtime when she chose to have one of her parents take the initiative and read her a story. But, even then, she called the shots: "Daddy, read it!" Paradoxically, though rebelliousness may be born of this boundary testing, so too is structure and security. Even as the child transgresses external boundaries, she is building internal boundaries that will define her sense of self. While the limits imposed by others may be broken in the name of freedom—one's capacity to decide things for oneself rather than simply suffer the decisions made by others—one is simultaneously affirming one's being-for-oneself *and* one's being-for-others. This dual impulse governs our lives beyond childhood, finding expression in the search for a wider self, new horizons, new beginnings, and what Karl Jaspers calls the Encompassing (*das Umgreifende*)—"the ultimate Being which is the foundation of our concepts but which can never be exhaustively grasped by them."[10] There is thus a dialectic between the orgiastic profligacy of the young and the pacific reveries of the old, and both Dionysian excess and Apollonian constraint are at play in every human situation as we struggle to reconcile the inner imperatives of our own existence and the entrenched, normative demands of a world that precedes, surrounds, and outlasts us.

Negotiating this uncertain relationship between mundane and extra-mundane realms is, arguably, the *fons et origo* of what we call religion, though cross-cultural comparison is only possible if we find a vocabulary that speaks to what is existentially *there* before we invoke words like *religion*, *ecology*, or *culture* to define it. Paul Ricoeur writes of what is "always-already present" before we have a name for it, inchoate experiences that precede or elude dates and definitions.[11] For Ricoeur, this is "the enigma of anteriority"—the mystery of how we might understand "potency" before we speak of potentates or powers-that-be, how we might understand "religion" before we speak of specific creeds or traditions, how we might understand "love" before we distinguish between eros and agape. But how is it possible to speak of such diffuse and unnameable phenomena? Carl Jung's phenomenology begins not with the names we give to things, but with "occurrences, events, experiences—in a word, with facts."[12] Moreover, Jung says, certain facts of experience are common to people everywhere, whatever their historical, cultural, or personal situations. Such experience, he argues, is captured in Rudolf Otto's notion of the *numinosum*, "that is, a dynamic agency or effect not caused by an arbitrary act of will. On the contrary, it seizes and controls the human subject who is always rather its victim than its creator." Not only does this force defy our ability to control or name it; it manifests itself in so many ways that it would be foolish for us to decide which are, in essence, "religious" or "secular," "real" or "imagined."

Ricoeur avows, moreover, that he is not concerned with Spinoza's "theology." Spinoza's alleged pantheism or atheism is irrelevant; only the notion of *conatus* matters. In this sense, "God is Life."[13] But life is more than the impulse to passively "persevere in being"; it consists in the search for "adequate ideas" that enable us to *actively* sustain our sense of presence and purpose.[14] God is but one of such ideas, and its adequacy consists in its ability to help us realize our capacity for speaking, acting, praying, and even narrating our story.[15] To submit to a higher power is not, therefore, to forfeit one's own agency *but to recover it through a relationship with something beyond oneself*, be this a supportive friend, a divinity, a diviner, or a material object. Here the divine and the utopian coalesce as alternative symbols of what William James calls "the more." For we are all susceptible to the uneasy sense "that there is *something wrong about us* as we naturally stand," and what we call religion is a set of ideas and practices for getting in touch with an "elsewhere," an "otherness," or a "wider self" that lies beyond the horizons of one's immediate lifeworld, especially at times when our "lower being has gone to pieces in the wreck."[16] This process of othering, which places one's own agency in abeyance, is a precondition for clearing one's head of confusing subjective preoccupations and returning to oneself as someone capable of taking a hand in determining his or her own fate.

## The Top Five Regrets of the Dying

In 2011 an Australian palliative care nurse published an account of the regrets that individuals had confided to her in the last days of their lives. In these rueful epiphanies one discerns a human need to live life on one's own terms. We also see how difficult it is to overcome the anxieties and resistances that stand in the way of crossing the frontier from what is tried and true to what makes sense *for oneself.* "I wish I'd had the courage to live a life true to myself, not the life others expected of me. I wish I hadn't worked so hard. I wish I'd had the courage to express my feelings. I wish I had stayed in touch with my friends. I wish that I had let myself be happier."[17]

How universal are these variations on the theme of finding fulfillment outside any prescribed or circumscribed order?

If we remember that individuation always involves "I" and "we" aspects, then all our actions have repercussions for ourselves *and* for others, regardless of whether they are construed as self-serving or altruistic, rebellious or conformist. Moreover, in all societies people seek, and are encouraged, to live as if more than their own fate depends on what they say and do. Whether the common good or the good of the individual is invoked as justification for any act, neither goal can be achieved unless people act and speak as if their own lives *and* the life of the world were contingent upon their decisiveness. Even maintaining the world as one finds it—which is ostensibly the goal of traditional societies—would be impossible if people did not act mindfully and determinedly in pursuit of that end.

Accordingly, every human being must live for his own reasons, rather than under duress. To act *as if* the world were in a sense *their* world, and they were not mere hostages to some transcendent reality. This implies that one must live, to some extent, against the grain of the given world if one's own world is to emerge and the vitality of *the* world thereby renewed. J. K. Rowling put it this way in her 2013 Harvard commencement address. "It is impossible to live without failing at something, unless you live so cautiously that you might as well not have lived at all—in which case, you fail by default. . . . The knowledge that you have emerged wiser and stronger from setbacks means that you are, ever after, secure in your ability to survive. You will never truly know yourself, or the strength of your relationships, until both have been tested by adversity."

For Kuranko, the village sets limits, while the bush offers limitless possibilities. The bush is a metaphor for the vitality without which one's own life becomes pointless and the life of the village dies. From a cybernetic point of view, any social system—defined as a domain of ascribed roles, inflexible rules, ancestral values, and received wisdom—drifts toward entropy unless it perennially taps into and draws upon the "wild" energies of the bush—the fertility of its soil, its regenerative resources, and even the *genii loci* who may bestow on a chosen individual supernatural powers. This is why African migrants commonly speak of Europe as a symbolic "bush"—a place that offers the hope of regeneration, and "a future" that is not simply a repetition of the past. And this is why the Revolutionary United Front that laid waste to Sierra Leone in the 1990s so strongly identified with the bush, locating its camps in the forests and deploying symbols of hunting and initiation to reinforce in child soldiers their rebellion against established authority.[18] But "wild" power is ambiguous. Though it may give an individual a sense of being fully alive, it can ruin a marriage, destroy a friendship, and tear a community apart. Clearly, fulfillment is never an either/or matter—a question of blind obedience or unfettered freedom. A balance must be struck between the 'I' and the "we": between one's own imperatives and the imperatives of living with others.

## Life Is Elsewhere

My Sierra Leone fieldwork affirmed an existential view that human life is meaningless unless we can contrive to transform the given world into a world we feel that we chose, that we can call our own. Charlotte Brontë put it perfectly in *Jane Eyre*.

> It is in vain to say human beings ought to be satisfied with tranquillity: they must have action; and they will make it if they cannot find it. Millions are condemned to a stiller doom than mine, and millions are in silent revolt against their lot. Nobody knows how many rebellions besides political rebellions ferment in the masses of life which people earth. Women are supposed to be very calm generally: but women feel just as men feel; they need exercise for their faculties, and a field for their efforts,

as much as their brothers do; they suffer from too rigid a restraint, too absolute a stagnation, precisely as men would suffer; and it is narrow-minded in their more privileged fellow-creatures to say that they ought to confine themselves to making puddings and knitting stockings, to playing on the piano and embroidering bags. It is thoughtless to condemn them, or laugh at them, if they seek to do more or learn more than custom has pronounced necessary for their sex.[19]

Mikhail Bakhtin recognized this existential protest against fixed ascriptions of status, role and hierarchical order in his notion of the carnivalesque, while Henri Bergson saw the celebration of organic life as an *élan vital* that resists the mechanistic routines of everyday life and allows for individual creativity and freedom. More recently, Mattijs van de Port has described the bacchanalian exuberance and excess of Serb townsmen's forays to Roma bars where frenzied music, "obscene songs, drunkenness, surrender, extravagance and the complete rejection of Novi Sad's renowned bourgeois respectability" suggests that though Roma are stigmatized as unclean, uncouth, and unmarriageable they also provide a refuge from lives claustrophobically encased "in the rules, conventions and standard of decency prescribed by the bourgeois ideals of civilization." Within the European social imaginary, the "Gypsy camp was an erogenous zone, the closest wildness, invested with unfulfilled desires, impossible yearnings and unsatisfied passions."[20]

This vitalist strain not only finds expression in Western *lebensphilosophie*, from Schopenhauer and Nietzsche to Bataille and Deleuze; it has analogues in traditional African thought.

Life is elsewhere—in a place remote from where I am. Though the wilderness is fraught with danger, it is also the source of regenerative power. Among the Sukuma-Nyamwezi of western Tanzania the wilderness is a place of witches and sorcerers who would destroy *mhola* (the social order), "but this is also where the child-bearing wife and the rain-giving king come from; and this is also where men, hit by the disaster of *nzala*, starvation, move to find new sources of food."[21]

Curiously, too, the most distant may best articulate moral ideals. If the gods and ancestors who embody these ideals are to possess real power and command respect, they must be otiose—at one remove from the human world. Familiarity is incompatible with authority. Sukuma-Nyamwezi thought is again illuminating: "The figure of the rain-bearing king and the figure of the child-bearing wife both symbolically derive their regenerative power from their metonymical relationship with wilderness and the world of strangers."[22] Freed from the snares and ambiguities of the immediate life-world, remote and imagined worlds can promise possibilities that cannot be realized closer to home.

But there is a catch. The greater the distance between humans and the gods, the more problematic becomes communication between them. In practice, therefore, a kind of counterpoint or tension usually exists between sacerdotal communication (in which priests keep ordinary mortals at a distance from their gods or divine kings) and mystical communication (in which direct, unregulated, spontaneous union between mortals and immortals is possible).

Just as gods and ancestors are foci of ambivalent feelings (provoking anxiety if they become too distant or too familiar), so too are exotic and distant places. For insular Europe, the sea and the sea voyage were for centuries the prevailing metaphors for this hunger for self-realization and riches in the beyond.[23] Like El Dorado and Shangrila in the West, one hears rumors among the Kuranko of a fabulous town somewhere in the hazy savannah regions to the northeast, known as Musudugu—town of women—where there are no men, where women are in possession of the most powerful Kuranko medicines and means of sorcery, and where great wealth may be gained. At once attainable and out of reach, the quasi-mythical Musudugu brings to mind the paradox of all power: that it must be theoretically accessible yet at the same time practically so scarce as to be almost impossible to access.

Consider the Azande, whose most powerful oracle (*benge*) originated outside Zandeland and, at the time E. E. Evans-Pritchard lived among them, had to be sought in arduous two-hundred-kilometer journeys, subject to strict taboos and frontier controls, to the Bomokandi River in the Belgian Congo. When asked why they did not cultivate the poison creeper in their own country and so save themselves the trouble of gathering it under such hazardous conditions, Zande informants expressed "disapproval" of the question, alleging that a kinsman would die if this were done. "We may suppose," observed Evans-Pritchard, "that the mystical potency of the poison is derived partly from its scarcity and the pains that must be expended in procuring it."[24] But the power of the alien lies in its essential otherness, not simply its scarcity. As in medieval philosophy, *alteritas* connotes not only otherness but the possibility of transcendence. That which is furthest from my grasp and control is that which poses the greatest existential threat to my being. By making that foreign thing my own, by assimilating it to myself, by incorporating it within my being, by bringing it under my control, I disarm its menace. But, more significantly, the existential blood, sweat, and tears that go into the taming of the alien object come to imbue the object. In this way its power objectifies my power over the other. That which was alien now stands to augment rather than diminish me.

There is another aspect to this fascination with alterity. It is as if every society, like every individual, is unable to sustain its existence as an isolate — can never be sufficient unto itself. As with the classical symbolon, human beings are driven to recover the side of themselves that gets lost, eclipsed, excluded, or denied in the formation of a normative system of thought or behavior. This occluded other is usually constructed as something inimical to the social order — a source of antisocial or wild power at the same time as it is a means of regaining lost personal autonomy and integrity. In short, it is construed simultaneously as a source of constructive and destructive energy.

I see no great difference between the Zande preference for the poison oracle over the termite oracle (the less potent oracle they used before they acquired *benge*) and the Western connoisseur's passion for tribal art, which, in its spurious exoticism, provides its owner with a vicarious shot of the libidinal energy and unbridled power, which, it is believed, primitives possess naturally.

# Dark Soundings

It's not always where and when you were born that matters; it's where you were reborn—when you were initiated into adulthood and with whom; when you walked away from an arranged or unfulfilling marriage; when you decided to quit a dead end job; when you left your natal village and risked your life crossing the borderlands to the global north; when you repudiated the genre conventions and assumptions that had framed your thinking for far too long. "I wanted to feel the blood running back into my veins, even at the cost of annihilation," writes Henry Miller, cutting his ties with America. "I wanted to shake the stone and light out of my system. I wanted the dark fecundity of nature, the deep well of the womb, silence, or else the lapping of the black waters of death. . . . Once you have given up the ghost, everything follows with dead certainty, even in the midst of chaos."[25] There are uncanny echoes here of Federico García Lorca's notion of the duende—that dark, soul-stirring force that surges up within us, drawing us beyond ourselves, into experiences that cannot be captured in words, but are conveyed in the dark sounds of flamenco, torn from the throat, "sweeping the earth with its wings made of rusty knives." "Where is the duende? Through the empty archway a wind of the spirit enters, blowing insistently over the heads of the dead, in search of new landscapes and unknown accents; a wind with the odor of a child's saliva, crushed grass, and medusa's veil, announcing the endless baptism of freshly-created things."[26]

New departures may not always involve forays into the wild, descents beneath the waters of an ocean or lake, journeys underground, or the violent overthrow of the social order. But they are all imagined in terms of death and rebirth.[27]

According to the earth-diver myths from the Americas, the world was originally a diffuse and insubstantial realm of sky and water that shared the same aqueous blueness. There is no earth. Nowhere a person can stand or settle.

Here is a Blackfoot variant of this myth.

Napioa, the Old Man, floated upon a log in the waters, and had with him four animals: Mameo, the fish; Matcekipis, the frog; Maniskeo, the lizard; and Spopeo, the turtle. He sent them down into the waters in the order named, to see what they could find. The first three descended, but never returned; the turtle, however, arose with his mouth full of mud. Napioa took the mud from the mouth of the turtle, rolled it around in the hollow of his hand, and in this manner made the earth, which fell into the waters, and afterward grew to its present size. There was only one person named Napioa. He lived in the world when the people who dwelt with him had two heads. He did not make these people, although he made the world, and how they came upon the earth no one knows. The Bloods do not know where Napioa came from. They do not know whether he was an Indian or not. He was not the ancestor of the Blackfeet, but the Creator of the Indian race. He was double-jointed. He is not dead, but is living in a great sea in the south. He did not make the white people, and the Indians do not know who made them.

Although we often dismiss such myths as prescientific speculations on how the world came into being and thereby see them solely as reflections of the culture in which they are found, myths speak to universal existential preoccupations that transcend the individual or social settings in which they first find expression.[28] Hence the argument that creation myths are allegories of ontogenesis. They obliquely recount the conditions under which every individual struggles to emerge, after a long gestation, from the undifferentiated ooze of life to become his own person—a creator rather than merely a creature of circumstance.

Freud observed that small children are often incredulous at the idea of birth from the vagina and imagine that the lump inside a woman's belly will pass from her body into the world in the same way that shit is excreted from the bowel via the anus. "The baby is produced like a piece of faeces."[29] This cloacal theory of birth is, however, not necessarily evidence of an infantile worldview. On the outlying Polynesian island of Bellona, the culture hero Ataganga began life alone, with no woman to marry. When he went to defecate, he felt something hard (or hard to excrete) in his feces. It was a small boy called Mauitikitiki. Ataganga adopted the boy as his son. A lazy and mischievous trickster, Mauitikitiki nonetheless proved his worth by fishing up Bellona's companion island of Rennel from the ocean depths.[30]

According to Maori oral traditions, Mauitikitiki also fished up the North Island of New Zealand (Te Ika-a-Maui, "the fish of Maui")—the island where I was raised. But this is not the only reason I find cloacal theories of birth plausible.

I am four years old. My sister and I are accompanying our mother on a day trip to see her friend Estelle. Estelle is married to a farmer, Cedric ("Ted") Corney, who has driven his truck to Inglewood to pick us up. Estelle and my mother were close friends at Wellington Teacher's Training College where they shared a passion for literature. After their marriages—Estelle to a farmer, my mother Emily to a bank clerk—they kept in touch.

After settling down with my mother at the kitchen table to drink a cuppa and catch up on news, Estelle orders her three-year-old son, Andrew, to show me around outside. Andrew leads the way to the milking shed where the cow bails and concrete floor have been hosed clean after the morning's milking. Adjoining the shed is a holding paddock in which there are two disused effluent sumps. I walk out into the paddock and approach what appears to be a concrete slab—the foundation of a demolished outhouse. I glance back. Andrew is standing by the shed, watching me. I step onto the slab. Solid is liquid, and I am falling blindly through ten feet of liquid manure. Dark clods and clouds bump and bruise me. An acrid ammoniac fluid invades my mouth. My feet touch bottom. Instinctively, I push off and flail upwards through slime and dung, my eyes scorched, my nostrils and throat scalded. The back of my wrist miraculously hits the edge of the concrete pit. I flip my hand over and grab hold. I haul myself out into the long grass, choking and shocked. I lie there like a drowned rat, drenched and seared by the reeking manure. A soft drizzle falls noiselessly over the farm. Andrew has not moved. The gap in the caked surface through which I plunged is already closing, the scum sealing its cracked lips. I run through the drizzle toward the house. Within minutes, I am in the bathroom, being helped out of my clothes. A large bathtub is slowly filling with cold water. Estelle is apologizing to my mother for what has happened and for the lack of hot water (the coal range that heats the water has not been lit). I sit in the shallow water, my bum on the cold enamel, shivering and vulnerable, still trying to clear my throat and nostrils of the dung.

As darkness falls, I sit huddled under a blanket on the tray of Ted Corney's truck as we jolt along the unsealed road. It seems to take ages to get home, though years later I will discover that the farm is only five miles from Inglewood. I fear that we are not going home at all but voyaging through the night to some other place altogether. Something has changed. But I have no conception of what it is or how I might speak of it.

Nowadays, I like to imagine this near-death experience as the origin of my aversion to bullshit—my distaste for pretension and prolixity, my quarrel with the academy, my contempt for those who "go along" with what others are doing simply because it is "the done thing." Perhaps, too, my early immersion in shit presaged a lifelong fascination with how value may be found in the most mundane and despised phenomena.

In 2012 Erika Eichenseer published a selection of German folktales that had been collected by a local historian Franz Xaver von Schönwerth in the Bavarian region of Oberpfalz at roughly the same time as the Grimm brothers were collecting their own now celebrated tales. Eichenseer called her selection *Prinz Roßwifl* (Prince Dung Beetle), because the wisdom contained in these (mainly) peasant stories could be compared to the precious cargo of eggs that the scarab beetle conceals in its ball of dung. One might also point out that the scarab beetle is a limitrophe creature par excellence, since it actually feeds upon the feces it gathers, while bringing nutrients to the environment in which it lives. In ancient Egypt the scarab was associated with Khepri, the god of the rising sun, both of whom were thought to create themselves out of nothing, hence the existential identification of the scarab with ontogenesis (coming into being) and the renewal of life.

In short, shit is not always bullshit.

Just as we translate pig into pork, sheep into mutton, and cow into beef to assist our pretense that we are not carnivorous killers, so, in farming parlance, shit is called manure. In the same way that meat and milk nourish us, manure fertilizes the pastures on which our cattle graze. In the years before the farming boom of the 1950s, Taranaki dairy farmers could not afford superphosphate, potash, or lime and depended on liquid manure to stimulate grass growth. This period was also the heyday of the compost clubs that pooled information on how to build a compost bin and produce the dark worm-infested loam in which vegetables would flourish, though local Maori had traditionally used compost in their kumara gardens, creating the phosphoric acids and potash salts that were lacking in many Taranaki soils.[31]

My father, who was an avid composter, would get barrow loads of horse manure from the sale yards half a mile from our house. I would help him shovel up the dung, marveling at its shape, and help him push the wheelbarrow home along the broken sidewalk, steadying it when it lurched or my father lost his footing. I shared his satisfaction as he created layers of horse manure, grass clippings, ash from our living room hearth, and organic refuse from the kitchen—an inedible version of the layer cakes my mother made for bring-and-buy stalls at the local flower show. So shit had its place in the scheme of things, and my perilous descent into that acrid and liquid darkness on Ted Corney's farm may have helped me acquire a life skill of getting myself out of the shit and finding in the most repellent experiences something of value, though I would never go as far as speaking of this experience as an "anal maternity" or declaring myself an "excremental anthropologist."[32]

## On Not Being Rule Governed

In revisiting my near-death experience, I found myself wondering what became of Andrew Corney, whom I had not seen or heard of since the early 1950s when we were Boy Scouts together. I failed to locate Andrew on the Internet, but I did find his sister Fleur, a celebrated writer of teenage fiction. I wrote to Fleur, asking if she could put me in touch with Andrew, only to learn that he had died of cancer in 2005. Fleur subsequently told me that Andrew's childhood passion had been building radio sets, and his first teacher had been my father's Radio Club pal, Dan Wilkinson. After graduating in science, Andrew specialized in metrology and became an internationally recognized specialist in AC calibration. But he never lost his love of amateur radio and was of the key figures in the famed Quartz Hill Radio Station on the wind-racked Wellington coast near Makara.

Through my email exchanges with Fleur, I felt reconnected with the country in which I had spent the first and formative years of my life. But I was struck by the paradox that I should now feel such a yearning for the place I could not wait to put behind me when I was twenty, convinced I had to reinvent myself elsewhere. Why should a country that I had once regarded as intellectually impoverished now seem, in my imagination, to be a source of replenishment and nourishment, while the country in which I had settled oppressed me as a rule-bound world in which I could not feel at home?

Much to my surprise, I found an answer to this question in one of Fleur's books—*I Am Not Esther.*

Ellen Pilgrim is raised in a fundamentalist Christian community called the Children of Faith. At sixteen she is raped by one of the elders, gets pregnant, and is ostracized from the community as a fallen woman. Ellen gives up her child for adoption and tries to make a new life for herself. At the time the novel begins, Ellen is dependent on her second child Kirby and losing her psychological battle to escape the hold of the Children of Faith over her. Under relentless pressure from her brother Caleb, who is a patriarch of the sect, Ellen tells her daughter that she is going to Africa to work with refugees and places her in Caleb's care. Grief-stricken and mystified by her mother's abandonment of her, Kirby suffers the ignominy of being obliged to answer to the biblical name of Esther, to discard her own clothes, pin up her hair, and submit to an Old Testament morality known as "The Rule." Kirby resists the "weird" disciplines of her new family and rails against her new identity. Placed in isolation for breaking The Rule, she "sat at the table and wrote, My Name is Kirby. I am not Esther. I was me. Not some robot they programmed." Ineluctably, however, through her bond with Daniel, a cousin who is already beginning to rebel against his family, and by caring for another cousin, a small and vulnerable girl, Kirby comes to accept her lot, and though she and Daniel finally flee the community and the wrath of Caleb, she finds herself wavering between the world into which she born and the world into which she had been thrown, "swinging between Esther and Kirby."

I read Fleur's novel as an allegory of childhood. On the one hand, we form deep attachments to our parents, who bring us into the world, care for us, and become our first role models. On the other hand, something in us cries out against simply repeating or perpetuating their lives. Or even doing what they tell us to do. We suffer what Harold Bloom called "the anxiety of influence."[33] We want to do things for ourselves, in our own way, in our own good time. To give birth to ourselves. To distance ourselves from their world, even though we may chose it later as our own.

When I wrote to Fleur, saying how affected I had been by her novel, I asked whether Kirby's experiences echoed her own in any way. "My own memories of a Taranaki childhood are very mixed," I said. "I felt happy and secure in a loving family, but a complete stranger to the town, which appeared to be inhabited by eccentrics, snobs, and bigots, and whose respectable facades concealed injustices and violence."

In response, Fleur told me that her husband had given her the idea for Esther. He had taught a boy from an Exclusive Brethren family that regarded education as evil, though the family was legally obliged to send its children to school until they were fifteen. "This boy wanted to be a doctor—argued with his father and got beaten up and kicked out of the family for refusing to comply. The door was slammed shut and he was told, 'Henceforth you are dead to us.' That story stayed in my head for about fifteen years until I felt it was time to write something based on it. (He did become a doctor—went to his mate's house and they took him in.) That struggle to be oneself is something I seem to visit fairly frequently—my other long-lasting book (*Slide the Corner*) is about a boy who has to fight his parents' determination that he follow their dreams, but he dreams of being a rally driver. The same theme pops up every few books, and I recognize that it springs from my childhood. Interestingly, not from the constraints of Inglewood so much—we were probably freer of that than you were since we were out in the country. Like you, we all couldn't wait to kick the mud of Inglewood off our boots—but, unusually for a farming family, both Mum and Dad were adamant that we'd get all the education possible and we all knew we'd leave Taranaki when we finished high school."

The parallelism between our stories was even more arresting when we shared recollections of our mothers' friendship. As Fleur put it, "Our mothers were very much fish out of water in Inglewood back in the fifties, and I know the friendship meant a lot to my mum. She used to make trips into Inglewood once a month to visit Emily."

Did their conversations ever turn to writing or to their shared love of literature? Throughout my childhood my mother would read us a chapter from a book after dinner—*Alice in Wonderland, The House at Pooh Corner, The Swiss Family Robinson, Gulliver's Travels*—and I would accompany her to the town library at least once a week. For Fleur, her mother "was key in me becoming a writer. She was always writing articles, plays, or stories—and every single night she would read to us and sometimes tell us stories she'd made up. She made words and story an integral part of my life. She had her first book published by Andre Deutsch in London in the seventies. It was called *Pa's Top Hat*—we were so proud of her."

## Confronting One's Demons

For several years following my traumatic experience on Ted Corney's farm, I suffered a recurring nightmare. I was alone on an iron-sand beach. It was neither day nor night, and the sea was a dark, ominous and magnetic presence, drawing me toward it. I tried to resist by clutching tufts of marram grass, holding onto a stone, digging my fingers into the sand. But nothing I did made any difference. The sea threatened to draw me into its dark maw. So terrified was I by this dream that I feared going to sleep. But one night, exhausted by my efforts to avoid a replay of the dream, I decided not to fight it any more, to accept my doom, to get it over with. The nightmares never recurred. They were replaced by dreams of levitation and of flying. If pursued by some demonic horde, I could, through sheer will power, rise above my pursuers and, in many cases, fly away from their clamoring hands.

Somehow I had stumbled on the trick of acting counterintuitively. It was akin to the technique of surviving a rip: resisting the desire to swim against the current, allowing yourself to be pulled out to sea, then swimming parallel to the shore until you are past the rip and able to use the inshore waves to regain the beach. In Kilton Stewart's controversial ethnography of Senoi dream therapy, a similar strategy is encouraged. Every morning, Senoi families participate in a 'dream clinic' in which the father and older brothers listen to and analyze the younger children's dreams. Often, a dreamer has been about to fall or be attacked by some hostile force. Rather than urge the dreamer to put the nightmare out of his mind, the analyst urges him to return to it the following night, and overcome his fear by allowing himself to fall or to engage with the force from which he fled in terror. The assumption is that "dream characters are bad only as long as one is afraid and retreating from them, and will continue to seem bad and fearful as long as one refuses to come to grips with them." Thus a Senoi analyst will say, "You must relax and enjoy yourself when you fall in a dream. Falling in the quickest way to get in contact with the powers of the spirit world, the powers laid open to you through your dreams. Soon, when you have a falling dream, you will remember what I am saying, and as you do, you will feel that you are traveling to the source of the power which has caused you to fall."[34]

The paradox of the limitrophe is that what is initially encountered as a minatory or punitive force may be transformed into a source of strength if one can summon the courage to embrace it.

A Kuranko story, related by a young man called Sulimani Koroma in the dry season of 1972, dramatically captures this theme.

The story is about a small hand drum called the yimbe that is played during initiations.

At the time the story begins, this yimbe drum is in the hands of the hyenas in the bush. But, hearing it night after night, the villagers become entranced by its sound and present an ultimatum to their chief: "If you do not bring the drum to us in the village, we will go into the bush." Concerned to keep the community together and maintain his authority, the chief promises a "hundred of everything" to anyone brave enough to bring the yimbe from the bush to the town.

A young man decides to try his luck. After saying good-bye to his mother—who fears she will not see her son again—he sets off on his quest. Deep in the bush, he encounters a cannibalistic djinn. But the djinn, impressed by the young man's audacity and courage, decides not only to spare his life but to help him by giving him a fetish, with instructions on how to address it in time of need, as well as an egg, a live coal, and a piece of bamboo.

That night the young man reaches the village of the hyenas. Though suspicious and wary, the hyenas offer him food and lodging and accede to his request to be allowed to sleep in the courthouse—where the yimbe drums are kept. In the middle of the night, he steals the sweetest-sounding yimbe and flees. Hyena Sira, the canniest of the hyenas, who has not slept for fear of what the young man might do, rouses the other hyenas and leads them in pursuit of the thief. However, each time the hyenas threaten to overtake him, the young man summons the fetish. The first time it tells him to throw down the bamboo, which becomes an impenetrable forest that hyena Sira has to gnaw her way through. The second time it tells him to use the live coal to set fire to the grass, though hyena Sira quickly douses the flames by pissing on them. The third time it tells him to throw down the egg; it turns into a great lake that enables the young man to reach the safety of the town with the yimbe drum in his possession.

Now the djinn had given the young man the fetish on condition that he kill a red bull and offer it as a sacrifice to the fetish when his quest was ended. But the young man forgets his promise, and when hyena Sira, disguised as a seductive young woman, comes to the village and entices him to accompany her home, he sets off with no thought for his safety.

Once they've crossed the lake, hyena Sira leads the young man into an ambush. As the hyenas close in for the kill, he shimmies up a tree and summons the fetish for help. The fetish says nothing. Desperately he summons it again. Again no response. It is then that he remembers his broken promise, and declares that he will sacrifice two bulls to the fetish if it saves him. As the hyenas are about to tear him limb from limb, the fetish breaks its silence. It tells him to take a branch from the tree. It turns into a gun. The fetish then tells him to take some leaves. These turn into bullets. He fires on the hyenas and they flee for their lives.

The young man returns home and makes the promised sacrifice to the djinn.

Three lessons may be drawn from this story. First, we owe our lives to others. As Maurice Merleau-Ponty puts it, "we are collaborators for each other in consummate reciprocity. Our perspectives merge into each other, and we coexist through a common world."[35] Second, the coherence and continuity of a community depends on *decisive individual acts*. Every person bears some responsibility for the society in which she lives. Third, our humanity is only fully realized when we suffer the ordeal of a second birth. In Kuranko initiation it is not the ordeal itself that possesses this transformative power; it is the neophyte's readiness to face the ordeal with equanimity and accept that joy and pain in life are mutually entailed. This is the burden of Nietzsche's motto, *increscunt animi, vivescit virtus* (the spirit grows, strength is restored by wounding), and of his view that "the value of a thing sometimes lies not in what one attains with it, but in what one pays for it—what it *costs* us."[36]

But what if the wounding is so great that we cannot recover from it? What if the value of the life we lose is never equivalent to the new life gained? What if the nightmare of history so overwhelms us that we lose all power to act or to speak?

## Renata

Historically, some of the most bitterly contested and battered provinces of Europe have been the limitrophe regions of Bohemia, Moravia, Transylvania, and Silesia. So when an ethnic German family of refugees arrived in Inglewood in 1950, I might have seen them—had I a better knowledge of the European century—as an embodiment of these tragic borderlands in which, often overnight, one's mother tongue is banned, one is obliged to speak another language, one's status goes from privilege to destitution, and one is forced, as the Kramers were, into a refugee camp because one has become persona non grata in the country one once called home (in their case, Silesia) and cannot return to the fatherland because it lies in ruins.

Clad in ill-fitting Red Cross clothing and footwear, they found no favor in our insular community, but when the daughter, whose name was Renata, joined our class, my heart went out to her. Though it was summer, she was dressed in a woolen skirt, rubber boots, and a threadbare jersey. Three years older than any of us, and speaking only broken English, she had endured privations I could only guess at, even years later when I tried to research her family's pre-antipodean life. Not only did the Kramers find themselves torn between Poland and Germany, and not "fully at home in either";[37] they discovered another no-man's-land between Europe and New Zealand that was even more deeply unsettling.

My abiding memory of Renata is her pallid beauty and the mood of sadness that hung over her like a cloud before falling as rain on the summer's day our class went to the school swimming baths and Renata emerged from the girl's bathing shed wearing a moth-eaten, old-fashioned woolen swimming costume that revealed her womanhood despite her brave attempts, by crossing her arms or placing one hand on her crotch, to conceal herself from our stares.

The Kramers rented a shabby council cottage opposite the railway station. Mr. Kramer worked as a street cleaner, and I would often see him chipping weeds with a hoe or cleaning a street gutter with a wire broom as I wended my way to school. Every Saturday night he and his wife would take their seats in the Town Hall and watch the same Hollywood movie I was watching, through very different eyes. Mrs. Kramer was much larger than her husband and was never seen without the fur coat she had brought with her from Europe. By contrast, her husband was a scrawny individual, always wearing the same worker's clothes and seemingly borne down by the weight of some great woe or weariness. When the lights came on at intermission, Mrs. Kramer would dispatch her husband to the Nibble Nook to buy a packet of Minties and an ice cream cone.

How is it, I ask myself now, sixty years later, that I am able to recall these details so vividly? How can I account for the fascination this foreign couple had for me? Or the sympathy I felt for Renata, whom I sometimes saw in her parents' company as they strolled around the town, perhaps repeating a habit formed in some refugee camp, of an evening promenade? Tony

Judt speaks of Europe's postwar history as "a story shadowed by silences; by absence."[38] Old communities, in which Catholics, Orthodox, Muslims, Jews, and others lived as neighbors, imploded and fragmented. "Thanks to war, occupation, boundary adjustments, expulsions and genocide, almost everybody now lived in their own country, among their own people."[39] But there were many, like the Kramers, who had no country to return to. Given such traumatic displacements and permanent losses, was it possible that Renata's real parents had been killed and that the Kramers had taken her in, perhaps to replace a child they had lost? And how had they survived the camps? Did Mrs. Kramer prostitute herself for the price of a loaf of bread, a slab of butter, a packet of sugar, a tin of bully beef? And what of Mr. Kramer during the war years, when his German ethnicity surely gave him privileges that Silesian Poles were systematically denied? What humiliations had he suffered? I have asked such questions for many years, knowing that they cannot be answered and also knowing that we inhabit the borderlands of history, shadowed by our previous lives and cursed by the indelible stain of things we did in order to survive.

One evening, Mr. Kramer came home from work and got into a slanging match with his wife. It would later transpire, from evidence heard at his trial, that these incomprehensible tirades were almost daily occurrences. According to Kramer's own testimony, his wife refused to endure another day in that hovel, that wretched town. Their lives were more degraded than they had been in the camps. He was not earning enough. He had let himself be defeated. He was weak. He was not man enough to fight for a better life for her or for Renata.

None of this I would ever have known had it not been for my grandfather, who was the local policeman in Inglewood for thirty-five years. Though he retired from the police force in 1946, he regularly visited his successor, and the two swapped stories, some of which were passed on to me.

Kramer did not respond to his wife's insults. He had heard it too many times before. He bided his time. He got up from his chair and walked without will or premeditation to the bathroom at the back of the house. He took his cutthroat razor, returned to the kitchen, and slit her throat.

He was tried in the New Plymouth Supreme Court, found guilty of manslaughter, and sentenced to twenty years' imprisonment. This was around 1953, when I was starting high school.

Renata disappeared from Inglewood, and from my life, forever.

I sometimes think that limitrophe describes not only geographical borderlands between one state and another but psychological borderlands between states of mind and between what passes for public knowledge and what is suppressed, salted away, never spoken of because it offends our self image or otherwise outrages our sense of who we are.

It is ironic that all my attempts to locate newspaper or archival records of the Kramer trial have come to nothing and that this murder never figures in accounts of Inglewood's violent past, though it would undoubtedly reinforce the popular claim that Inglewood is "the murder capital" and "psychopathic center" of New Zealand.

Statistics lend some support to this claim. While the national murder rate is about two per hundred thousand per annum, my hometown boasts a rate of twenty-five per hundred thousand—not alarming by U.S. standards (Inglewood, California has thirteen murders per thousand yet is safer than 25 percent of cities in the U.S.), but troubling for New Zealanders.[40] It isn't just the discrepancy between the pastoral appearance of my hometown and its hidden history of violence that is so mystifying; it is the brutal and bizarre forms this violence takes.[41] A boy brings a sawn-off .22 rifle to school and kills his teacher with a single shot to the head; a young man murders a couple with a knife, then severs their genitals and nails them to a wall; the members of a rugby team gatecrash a young man's twenty-first birthday party and sodomize him with a broom handle; the members of a local church beat a twelve-year-old boy's brains out with a concrete block in their zeal to rid him of the devil; a forty-seven-year-old woman with a gambling addiction seduces an elderly widower, then bashes him to death with a steam iron, puts his body in the trunk of her station wagon, and drives around the province, paying off her gambling debts by forging his signature on his checks.

When I was a boy my parents and grandparents were so determined to protect my innocence that such stories seldom reached my ears. But rumor—

like the shoots of the giant bamboos that grew wild in the backblocks of Taranaki—found a way through the cracks of even the best-defended homes. And as I grew older the national tabloid *Truth* was a source on which one could rely for the more salacious and vicious facts of life. Even though my high school did everything in its power to suppress publication of one of the worst crimes committed in its precincts, the story found its way into the pages of *Truth*, where I learned about the boys who, on a remote corner of the school farm, ganged up on another boy they disliked and castrated him with fencing pliers.

## Sentiments Limitrophes

Just as the Greek *nostos* is connected to the Indo-European root *nes*,[42] meaning return to light and life, so Maori imagine one's home place as a hearth where a fire is perpetually rekindled and kept burning (*ahi ka*).

Nostalgia was originally a medical diagnosis, characterized by "erroneous representations" that caused the afflicted to lose touch with present realities. The symptoms were allegedly identical to those of grief and mourning—hearing voices, seeing ghosts, dreaming of lost loved ones and localities, losing one's appetite, becoming immobile and depressed.[43]

There is, I believe, a close kinship between nostalgia and our yearning to know the truth about events that our parents and public authorities refuse to speak of. Our fascination with what is proscribed by censorship is not unlike our longing for the homeland from which we have become estranged.

For W. G. Sebald both these senses of being an outcast explained his attraction to out-of-the-way places, architectural anomalies, *objets trouvés* (particularly old postcards), and individuals who, so to speak, had been treated like shit.

> I do like to listen to people who have been sidelined for one reason or another. Because in my experience once they begin to talk, they have things to tell you that you won't be able to get from anywhere else. And I felt that need of being able to listen to people telling me things from very

early on, not least I think because I grew up in postwar Germany where there was—I say this quite often—something like a conspiracy of silence, i.e., your parents never told you anything about their experiences because there was at the very least a great deal of shame attached to these experiences. So one kept them under lock and seal. And I for one doubt that my mother and father, even amongst themselves, ever broached any of these subjects. There wasn't a written or spoken agreement about these things. It was a tacit agreement. It was something that was never touched on. So I've always . . . I've grown up feeling that there is some sort of emptiness somewhere that needs to be filled by accounts from witnesses one can trust. And once I started . . . I would never have encountered these witnesses if I hadn't left my native country at the age of twenty, because the people who could tell you the truth, or something at least approximating the truth, did not exist in that country any longer. But one could find them in Manchester, and in Leeds or in North London or in Paris—in various places, Belgium and so on.[44]

Sebald's reflections on displacement and marginality echo Henry Miller's remarks about his friend Alfred Perles. Miller describes Perles as having led so many lives, assumed so many identities, and acted so many parts that to do justice to his totality would be like reconstructing a jigsaw puzzle. "He lived continually *en marge.* He was 'limitrophe,' one of his favorite words, to everything, but he was not *limitrophe* to himself. In the first book he wrote in French (*Sentiments Limitrophes*) there were microscopic revelations of his youth which verged on the hallucinatory."[45]

## The Faraway Tree

In retrospect, my own past sometimes takes on hallucinatory qualities. I remember the woman in my hometown who bore a child out of wedlock and was the subject of perpetual gossip, her daughter as stigmatized as the mother, their house avoided as though it were haunted or held the power to pervert anyone who came too close to it . . . the woman who had been jilted in her youth and tried to commit suicide by throwing herself into a drowned quarry that served as the local rubbish tip, only to cripple herself for life, so that her painful limp was a sordid reminder to us all of the consequences of misguided passion . . . the school year that began with two weeks of soul-destroying military drill, marching hour after hour up and down an asphalt tennis court, forming ranks, right dressing, being ear bashed, bawled out, regimented, while in the heartbreaking distance one heard girl's voices from the gymnasium singing "Down in the Glen."

As a boy I clung to these remote, censured, or ostracized figures as if my life depended on them. And it was not insignificant that my closest friends were a Maori boy—Eddie Ngeru—and a new boy—David Derby-shire—whose passions for model airplanes, Arthur Ransom novels, and ir-reverent records by Spike Jones and Stan Freberg I also embraced with gusto. Though I was marking time on an outpost far from my true home, these outside influences sustained me and gave me glimpses into my future vocation as an ethnographer.

But it was the books I read that confirmed this sense that my real life lay elsewhere.

Until the 1960s, most children's books in New Zealand were imported from England. During the war years, and for some time after, these im-ports were restricted, so the few books we did acquire were precious to us. Among these were the faraway tree novels of Enid Blyton. This magical tree grew in an enchanted forest. Its upper branches were lost in the clouds, and small houses were built in its enormous trunk. When, years later, I read Italo Calvino's philosophical fable, *Il Barone Rampante* (The Baron in the Trees) and saw Rene Magritte's surrealist painting, *La Voix du Sang* (The Voice of Blood), I again felt the presence of an archetypal image that obliquely answers our yearning to be transported to a realm beyond the mundane one we actually inhabit. By dozing off on a summer's day, lapsing into reverie, falling down a rabbit hole, walking through the back of a ward-robe into a land of ice and snow, or being lulled into a trance by a parent reading a bedtime story, we instantly cross a threshold into another more nourishing world. Since many of the books I read as a child were English, it was inevitable that I would fantasize England as a land as hedgerows, friendly animals, and fabulous cities. One particular illustrated book, given to me on my seventh birthday by my mother and father, perfectly captured this mystery of elsewhere. *Mr. Mole's Tunnel*, told by Douglas Collins and pictured by G. W. Blackhouse, begins with the dilemma of Mrs. Mole, whose shopping expeditions to a town "on the sunny side of an enormous mountain" took "four hours to go, and five hours to come back".[46] The first illustration in the book shows Mrs. Mole trudging off from Shrew Hall to the train station. Four arms of a signpost point to "Station," "Faraway," "Nowhere," and "Someplace." Mrs. Mole decides that a move to Milesaway, on the sunny side of the mountain, is the only way of resolving the situation, but Mr. Moles is averse to moving and comes up with an ingenious plan for staying put *and* enabling his wife to travel to Milesaway in no time at all. *He would build a tunnel under the mountain.*

In this simple tale is captured one of humanity's oldest quandaries—how to be secure in some "dear perpetual place," yet, at the same time, able to draw sustenance from the world at large.

In reality, however, it is difficult to have it both ways. No magical wardrobes, rabbit holes, beanstalks, or tunnels, or even unmagical means of air travel, make it possible to *live* in two hemispheres. We are not godwits, who nest in one place and feed in another. We find ourselves divided between places we visit and the place we dwell. Only in one of these places can we keep the home fires burning. In the other places, memories dim, the fires die, the hearth grows cold.

Yet there is, perhaps, more irony in this dilemma than tragedy.

As a child, listening to the story of the Billy Goats Gruff, it never occurred to me that the risks they took in crossing the ogre-protected bridge to greener pastures would not pay off. Though the story ends with the reunited family trotting happily toward a lush meadow studded with wild flowers, it is perfectly possible that within a day of reaching this utopia one of the goats looked back to the other side of the river and noticed that the pastures they had abandoned actually looked greener than the pastures they had risked their lives to reach.

Though I was raised in a loving family, this did not prevent me from imagining that my friends' families might be more fun to live with.

Mrs. Derbyshire's meals were tastier than the meals my mother served. Eddie Ngeru's dilapidated house was more homely than my own. Even when I moved to a city, the promise of miraculous transformation was short-lived. The streets were not paved with gold, and no wealthy merchant's daughter fell in love with me or helped me make my fortune. For some reason my fantasizing reached an almost unbearable intensity when I was in an art gallery. It was not the paintings that carried me away, but the beautiful women I glimpsed as I moved from room to room. I came away from every visit to a gallery with an image of a dark and beautiful creature I would never have the courage to talk to, yet whose loss I would mourn for the rest of the day. Why is it that a girl glimpsed in passing, as from the window of a train, is always perfection, making the girl you actually love pale in comparison? As Montaigne, observed, "in love there is nothing but a frantic desire for what flees from us," and he cites Ariosto's lines on hunting:

> Just as a huntsman will pursue a hare
> O'er hill and dale, in weather cold or fair;
> The captured hare is worthless in his sight;
> He only hastens after things in flight.[47]

Why are we always reaching beyond that which we actually possess? Are we victims of mimetic desire—in which things take on value because others possess them and we do not? Or is it simply that distance lends enchantment—our imaginations forever migrating to somewhere over the rainbow or beyond the horizon, so that we live in the eternal hope that in giving up or giving away all we have known, all we have acquired, we instantly earn some fabulous favor or will receive some miraculous bounty?

It has taken me many years to realize that utopia can be anywhere and to understand that in looking for it elsewhere one risks destroying the possibility of ever finding it at one's feet. It may be that this unabated sense of mourning that rules my inner life explains the attraction I have felt for writers like Thomas Wolfe, D. H. Lawrence, James Joyce, W. G. Sebald, and Hannah Arendt, whose work attained its greatness in exile. And my own attenuated relationship with my native land may explain why I have always gravitated toward remote societies, drifters and derelicts, refugees, migrants, beached mariners, loners, and lost souls. Through these individuals, and in these places, I have found an oblique means of writing about my own alienation.

## What Lies Beneath

During the summer before I went to Sierra Leone, my wife and I would drive to Walden Pond every evening to walk or swim. By mid October the water was cold, and the woodland paths no longer crowded by pilgrims visiting the site of Thoreau's cabin. One utterly still evening, after walking the perimeter of the lake, we came upon eight figures standing strangely apart from one another at the water's edge, all looking toward the setting sun. As if answering an identical but inaudible summons, they held their iPads or Blackberries at arms length, like aliens making offerings to the western sky. But theirs was not some arcane ritual, but the all too human act of seeking to capture an experience that might be shared with others, posted on Facebook perhaps, with a single line of explanation—the implicit expression of a need to connect, to share what is in one's heart or on one's mind, and have it "liked." I was moved by these gestures against aloneness—faint images of the light fading from the sky and the black wall of oaks and pines where, like fireflies, the flash of cameras could be discerned, fitfully keeping a memory alive despite the shadows lengthening on the lake.

Can our words and concepts be compared with these fugitive images? Can we speak of limitrophes to language—regions of experience that lie outside the limits of what can be stated or claimed as states of mind? And does fiction—and by extension all forms of imaginative art—preserve a sense of these anterior realms that, despite our intellectual legerdemain, resist the rites of naming and knowing on which we set such store?

In 2010 the New York artist Michael Prettyman began translating *The Mahabharata* from the original Sanskrit and creating images to accompany the text. Classically trained, and mindful that most religious imagery is figurative—four-armed Vishnu, winged angels, Jesus with his halo, the

Buddha blissful in lotus position — Michael's first attempts conformed to tradition. But the results were, to his mind, kitsch, and he experimented with other ways of doing justice to the text. One of his teachers had emphasized the monistic aspect of Hinduism, and Michael now decided that a more abstract approach was called for, a process that would involve subtraction rather than addition, that would strip away the outward forms of religious iconography or religious language in order to touch upon that which eluded conventional depictions and representations. Michael had learned that the black surface of unexposed film conceals all the colors of the spectrum. So he purchased a large sheet of photo-sensitive paper and exposed it to the night sky. He then tried various solvents, hoping they would dissolve the surface and reveal what lay beneath. His wife suggested using caustics. He added acids to his repertoire, spilling chemicals on the black emulsion and discovering abstract forms that evoked, in their randomness and unpredictability, cosmic truths that are usually obscured if not completely masked by conventional forms of expression. When Michael spoke to me about this project he cited something Picasso wrote in 1923. "Among the several sins that I have been accused of committing, none is more false than the one that I have, as the principal objective in my work, the spirit of research. When I paint, my object is to show what I have found and not what I am looking for. In art intentions are not sufficient and, as we say in Spanish, love must be proved by facts and not by reasons."[48]

## Schrödinger's Cat

At the Boston airport I found myself standing behind a woman in her thirties. The woman's daughter wore wire-framed spectacles and had a pink suitcase. I guessed her to be about ten. An older woman, who I thought at first to be unrelated to the mother and daughter, turned out to be the child's grandmother. The younger woman was holding a paperback called *Who's Afraid of Schrödinger's Cat?* When she and her mother exchanged a few words, I got the impression that the grandmother was English, but the accent of the woman with the paperback was unstable — American one second, British the next. It was then that I remembered that in Schrödinger's quantum world there is no either/or. Many possibilities, including contradictory ones, coexist. One can be dead and alive at the same time. One can be simultaneously living out two different destinies or be a member of two different generations. Self and other are not opposed; they are the same person realized in different aspects. Everything depends on the position, place, and point of view from which one makes one's observations. In the words of Fernando Pessoa, *each of us is several, is many, is a profusion of selves. So that the self who disdains his surroundings is not the same as the self who suffers or takes joy in them. In the vast colony of our being there are many species of people who think and feel in different ways.*[49]

# Notes

1. *Barawa, Or The Ways Birds Fly in the Sky: An Ethnographic Novel* (Washington: Smithsonian Institution Press, 1986); *At Home in the World* (Durham: Duke University Press, 1995); *The Blind Impress* (Palmerston North: Dunmore, 1997); *In Sierra Leone* (Durham: Duke University Press, 2004); *Road Markings: An Anthropologist in the Antipodes* (Dunedin: Rose Mira, 2012).

2. Jacques Derrida, "This Strange Institution Called Literature," in *Acts of Literature*, ed. D. Attridge (London: Routledge, 1992), 73.

3. Jacques Derrida, "Deconstruction and the Other," interview with Richard Kearney, in *Dialogues with Contemporary Continental Thinkers: The Phenomenological Heritage*, ed. Richard Kearney (Manchester: Manchester University Press, 1984), 105–126 (116, 117).

4. One of the surprises of the Human Genome Project was the discovery that the human genome contains only twenty to twenty-five thousand protein-coding genes, about a fifth the number researchers had expected to find. To search for the missing pieces that could account for this discrepancy, researchers started looking toward other sources of genetic material that contribute to human function. One of these sources was the human microbiome—defined as the collective

genomes of the microbes (composed of bacteria, bacteriophage, fungi, protozoa, and viruses) that live inside and on the human body. We have about ten times as many microbial cells as human cells, and an analysis of the full gene content and composition of these microbiomes (i.e., the metagenome) predicts that there may be more than eight million unique microbial genes associated with the microbiomes across the human body of these healthy adults. When compared to the total number of human genes, this suggests that the genetic contribution of the microbiome to the human supraorganism may be many hundreds of times greater than the genetic contribution from the human genome. Joy Yang, "The Human Microbiome Project: Extending the Definition of What Constitutes a Human," www.genome.gov/27549400.

5. Gloria Anzaldúa, *Borderlands/La Frontera: The New Mestiza* (San Francisco: Aunt Lute, 1999), 101.

6. Davíd Carrasco, "Desire and the Frontier: Apparitions from the Unconscious in The Old Gringo," in *The Novel in the Americas*, ed. Raymond Leslie Williams (Boulder: University of Colorado Press, 1992), 102.

7. Frederick Jackson Turner, *The Frontier in American History* (New York: Holt, 1920), 293.

8. Michael Jackson, "The Kuranko: Dimensions of Social Reality in a West African Society," PhD diss., University of Cambridge, 1971, viii–xi.

9. Joe Simpson, *Touching the Void* (London: Vintage, 1997), 214–215.

10. William Earle, "Introduction," *Reason and Existenz: Five Lectures by Karl Jaspers*, trans. William Earle (Milwaukee: Marquette University Press, 1997), 10.

11. Paul Ricoeur, *Critique and Conviction: Conversations with François Azouvi and Marc de Launay*, trans. Kathleen Blamey (New York: Columbia University Press, 1998), 98–100.

12. Carl Jung, "Psychology and Religion," in *Psychology and Religion: West and East*, trans. R. F. C. Hull (Princeton: Princeton University Press, 1969), 6.

13. Paul Ricoeur, *Oneself as Another*, trans. Kathleen Blamey (Chicago: University of Chicago Press, 1992), 315. Cf. William James: "Does God really exist? How does he exist? What is He? are so many irrelevant questions. Not God, but life, more life, a larger, richer, more satisfying life is, in the last analysis, the end of religion." *The Varieties of Religious Experience: A Study in Human Nature* (New York: Signet, 1958), 382.

14. Ricoeur, *Oneself as Another*, 316.

15. "What I find intriguing about Spinoza's notion of *conatus*," Ricoeur writes, "is that it refuses the alternative between act and potency. . . . For Spinoza, each concrete thing or event is always a mélange of act and possibility." And this defines the field of ethics. Ricoeur, "The Power of the Possible," in Richard Kearney, *Debates in Continental Philosophy: Conversations with Contemporary Thinkers* (New York: Fordham University Press, 2004), 44.

16. James, *The Varieties of Religious Experience*, 383–384.

17. Bronnie Ware, *The Top Ten Regrets of the Dying: A Life Transformed by the Dearly Departing* (New York: Hay House, 2011).

18. Michael Jackson, "Custom and Conflict in Sierra Leone," in *Lifeworlds: Essays in Existential Anthropology* (Chicago: Chicago University Press, 2013), 125–126.

19. Charlotte Brontë, *Jane Eyre* (New York: Dutton, 1908), 105.

20. Mattijs van de Port, *Gypsies, Wars, and Other Instances of the Wild: Civilization and its Discontents in a Serbian Town* (Amsterdam: Amsterdam University Press, 1998), 5, 7.

21. Per Brandström, "Seeds and Soil: The Quest for Life and the Domestication of Fertility in Sukuma-Nyamwezi Thought and Reality," in *The Creative Communion: African Folk Models of Fertility and the Regeneration of Life*, ed. Anita Jacobson-Widding and Walter van Beek (Stockholm: Uppsala Studies in Cultural Anthropology 15, 1990), 178.

22. Ibid., 181.

23. Hans Blumenberg, *Shipwreck with Spectator*, trans. Steven Rendall (Cambridge: MIT Press, 1997).

24. E. E. Evans-Pritchard, *Witchcraft, Oracles, and Magic Among the Azande* (Oxford: Clarendon, 1937), 271.

25. Henry Miller, *Tropic of Capricorn* (New York: Grove, 1961), 76.

26. Frederico García Lorca, "Theory and Play of the Duende," trans. A. S. Kline, www.poetryintranslation.com/PITBR/Spanish/LorcaDuende .htm. According to some etymologies, the word *duende* derives from *duen de casa*, lord of the house. It is a capricious household spirit, depicted in folklore as a little boy or old man, who sometimes plays tricks on the householders, sometimes helps them with their chores. Jennifer Sime, "Exhumations: The Search for the Dead and the Resurgence of the Uncanny in Contemporary Spain," *Anthropology and Humanism* 38, no 1: 36–53 (48).

27. As Bataille puts it, "myth is identified not only with life but with the loss of life—with degradation and death." Georges Bataille, *Visions of Excess: Selected Writings, 1927–1939*, ed. Allan Stoekl (Minneapolis: University of Minnesota Press, 1985), 82.

28. For Lévi-Strauss, the origin of myth lies in the unconscious structuring processes of the human mind, in which case, he writes, "it is immaterial whether . . . the thought processes of the South American Indians take shape through the medium of my thought, or whether mine take place through the medium of theirs." Claude Lévi-Strauss, *The Raw and the Cooked*, trans. John and Doreen Weightman (London: Jonathan Cape, 1970), 13. The case for the psychoanalytic view that "mythology is psychology projected upon the external world" has been eloquently argued by Dundes. Alan Dundes, "Earth-Diver: Creation of the Mythopoeic Male," *American Anthropologist* 64, no. 5 (October 1962): 1032–1051 (1037).

29. Sigmund Freud, *A General Introduction to Psycho-analysis* (New York: Permabooks, 1953), 328. For analogous fantasies and myths of anal birth, see Dundes, "Earth-Diver," 1038–1040.

30. Samuel H. Elbert and Torben Monberg, *From the Two Canoes: Oral Traditions of Rennel and Bellona* (Honolulu: University of Hawaii Press, 1965), 112–113.

31. L. Bishop, "A Note on the Composition of a Maori Compost from Taranaki," *Journal of the Polynesian Society* 33, no. 4 (1924): 317–320.

32. Bataille, *Visions of Excess*, 85. I allude here to André Breton's denunciation of Georges Bataille as an "excremental philosopher" (in his 1929 *Second Surrealist Manifesto*), undoubtedly a comment on the latter's anal obsessions and "excremental fantasies." Allan Stoekl, "Introduction," in Bataille, *Visions of Excess*, xi.

33. Harold Bloom, *The Anxiety of Influence: A Theory of Poetry* (New York: Oxford University Press, 1975).

34. Kilson Stewart, "Dream Therapy in Malaya," in *Altered States of Consciousness*, ed. Charles T. Tart (New York: Wiley, 1969), 159–167 (163, 162).

35. Maurice Merleau-Ponty, *Phenomenology of Perception*, trans. Colin Smith (London: Routledge and Kegan Paul, 1962), 354.

36. Friedrich Nietzsche, *Twilight of the Idols*, trans. R. J. Hollingdale (Harmondsworth: Penguin, 1968), 21, 92.

37. Karl Cordell and Stefan Wolff, "Ethnic Germans in Poland and the Czech Republic: A Comparative Evaluation," in *Nationalities Papers: The Journal of Nationalism and Ethnicity* 33, no. 2 (2005): 255–276 (272).

38. Tony Judt, *Postwar: A History of Europe Since 1945* (New York: Penguin, 205), 8.

39. Ibid., 9.

40. Graeme Lay, "Murder in Moaville," electronic document, http://quote unquotenz.blogspot.com/2010/07/graeme-lay-on-inglewood.html.

41. In one cross-cultural research project, individuals aged sixteen to eighteen from eleven different countries were assigned tasks involving such contentious issues as an unfaithful spouse, a romantic triangle, disciplining a child, a public dispute, conflict at work, international conflict, etc. and asked to write an imaginative story about how characters in these situations will respond to conflict. Potential solutions ranged from violent to nonviolent. The highest frequency of violent responses was found among New Zealanders. Dane Archer

and Patricia McDaniel, "Violence and Gender: Differences and Similarities Across Societies," in *Interpersonal Violent Behaviors: Social and Cultural Aspects*, ed. R. Barry Ruback and Neil Alan Weiner (New York: Springer, 1995), 63–87.

42. Svetlana Boym, *The Future of Nostalgia* (New York: Basic Books, 2001), 7.

43. Ibid., 3–5.

44. Michael Silverblatt, "A Poem of an Invisible Subject," interview with W. G. Sebald, in *The Emergence of Memory: Conversations with W. B. Sebald*, ed. Lynne Sharon Schwartz (New York: Seven Stories, 2010), 84–85.

45. Henry Miller, *Remember to Remember* (London: Grey Walls, 1952), 191.

46. Douglas Collins, *Mr. Mole's Tunnel* (London: Collins, 1946).

47. Michel de Montaigne, "Of Friendship," in *The Complete Essays of Montaigne*, trans. Donald M. Frame (Stanford: Stanford University Press, 1958), 137.

48. Cited in *Futurism à Paris*, ed. Didier Ottinger (Paris: Centre Pompidou: 5 Continents, 2008), 311.

49. Fernando Pessoa, *The Book of Disquiet*, trans. Richard Zenith (Harmondsworth: Penguin, 2003), 327–328.

# Part Two

# Harmattan

**Harmattan** [f. Fanti or Tshi (W. Africa) haramata.]
A dry parching land-wind, which blows during December, January, and February, on the coast of Upper-Guinea; it obscures the air with a red dust-fog.

—*Shorter Oxford English Dictionary*

## Stories Happen

For many years I've been trying to track down a phrase I originally associated with Thucydides—"stories happen to people with stories to tell." The closest I got was a line from the last volume of Paul Auster's *New York Trilogy*—"stories only happen to those who are able to tell them." I would not mind if the phrase I had carried in my head for twenty years before *The New York Trilogy* was published turned out to be a garbled version of something Paul Auster wrote, for his preoccupation with shape-shifting was also mine—the curious way in which individuals and their stories metamorphose, each borrowing its identity from elsewhere and leaving us perennially uncertain as to whether we are the authors of our own lives and who is the "real" author of any story told. There's another line, attributed to Henry James, that is also pertinent: "For any writer there is the story of one's hero, and then, thanks to the intimate connection of things, the story of one's story itself." I have never been able to confirm this attribution either, and have concluded that my failure to determine the source of the two quotations I wanted to use as epigraphs for this book is an oblique proof of the point both make about our vagrant identities and the difficulty of staying true to anyone or to any one idea.

## Thousands Bay

On January 6, 1999, Freetown was invaded by a rebel force that moved through the city at will, seeking out those with whom the insurgents had a score to settle, plundering homes and government buildings, killing whoever stood in its way. Dressed in a motley of army fatigues and bizarre accessories—World War II helmets, gas masks, wigs, Santa Claus hats—and carrying AK-47 assault rifles or rocket-propelled grenade launchers, the insurgents rampaged as far as the West End before being turned back by Nigerian troops. In the midst of this mayhem, my friends Braima and Aisha disappeared. That they were murdered was not in question. But how they died I did not know, and when I allowed myself to picture the gruesome circumstances of their deaths something in me died too.

As I picked my way along an eroded laterite lane between shanties of rusted tin, a man with a toothbrush in his hand watched me from the verandah of his house, then spat a gout of toothpaste and saliva onto the red earth.

Braima's house was on the edge of a tidal inlet, isolated from the corrugated iron shanties of the quarter by a concrete wall topped with glass shards.

When I banged my fist on the iron gate, a disgruntled watchman in bare feet unlocked two padlocks, drew back the bolt, and let me in without asking who I was.

Crossing the compound of the gutted and ransacked home, I was choking back tears—for I had imagined that in making this pilgrimage I might feel Braima's and Aisha's presence again, commune with their spirits, or even find them still alive. Instead, I encountered a pockmarked facade with black holes where windows had once been, broken glass underfoot, a strip of torn curtaining, and saplings growing through the cracked concrete slab.

Without asking for the watchman's name, or questioning his vigil over this place of ruination, I dashed him before proceeding down the path to the inlet. Some women were beating sudsy garments against boulders and gossiping breathlessly. Out on the water a solitary fisherman stood in the slip of his canoe, poling slowly toward the Aberdeen Bridge where scores of rebel soldiers were brought in January 1999, summarily shot, and their bodies thrown into the bay.

It was almost dusk when I finally left the inlet and headed back toward the main road. I did not look back at the house, but took one last look at the estuary. The tide was going out, and women and children were searching for shellfish on the exposed mudflats.

I remembered an evening, long ago, when I sat with Aisha on the balcony, gazing at this very scene, and Aisha told me that it was from here that the slave ships set sail for the Americas with their human cargoes. Though the bay was called Thompson's Bay, its original name was Thousands Bay, she said, because of the thousands of doomed people who were confined in barracoons along the foreshore before being herded in chains into longboats to begin their middle passage to the New World.

As the bluish twilight settled over the mangroves and the mudflats, I found myself thinking how easily scenes of horror and tranquillity succeed each other on the same stage and I recalled Conrad's *Heart of Darkness*, where the narrator, watching the light fading on a sea-reach of the Thames, turns to his companions and declares, *this also has been one of the dark places of the earth.*

## Persona Non Grata

When a battered Nissan, belching blue smoke, stopped for me, I collapsed into a broken vinyl seat and closed my eyes. Did I have the emotional resources to make my planned journey to Barawa? And what would I find there? The war was over, but I doubted whether a new beginning lay in store for me. I was in half a mind to order my taxi driver to return me to Lungi Airport, but instead I fell into a desultory conversation about the difficulties of everyday life in Sierra Leone. His name was Mobutu. He had been a baker before the war. Now he drove a taxi. "We are really struggling here," he said, and went on to describe what he called "the work situation." There were two kinds of jobs, he explained—black man's jobs and white man's jobs. The first were like the jobs you get in Europe, where you receive a regular salary. The second were menial, transitory, and underpaid. Mobutu had tried to get a job with the UN, but had been told that only drivers who could read and write need apply. He had never attended school and bemoaned the fact that literacy counted for more than driving skills.

That night, ensconced in the old colonial bungalow I'd rented at Fourah Bay College, the smell of mildew, varnish, and decaying foliage conspired to blur the line between present and past. As I fell asleep, I tried to conjure an image of my wife in Lexington, going for her evening walk around Walden Pond without me. But it was Braima who sprang to mind. I was sitting opposite him at a long table, playing one of the tapes I had made in Barawa and pressing the stop button from time to time to ask my friend to explain an arcane allusion or obscure word.

On my second evening, I strolled down to the guest house to buy a beer. The bar was filled with disgruntled college lecturers who had completed degrees in Europe or the U.S. only to return home to paltry salaries, degraded facilities, an outdated library, and students whose inflated expectations they could not possibly hope to meet. The only other non-African in the bar was a young Englishman about to embark on doctoral research in Kono. Though older than my son, I felt a fatherly concern for the young man, though disguising this as academic curiosity in what he proposed to research and an offer of practical advice on the region in which he would be working. But Tom Lannon made it very clear that he not only knew what he was doing; he wanted to do it in his own way and in his own time, as if accepting help might later detract from the singularity of his achievement.

I inquired what college he was at.

"Johns," the Englishman said curtly.

"I did my doctorate at Churchill. Many moons ago."

Lannon showed no interest.

"Are you living on campus?" I asked.

"No," Lannon said, "I'm staying downtown with a friend."

*O youth! The strength of it, the faith of it, the imagination of it!* I saw no point in continuing the conversation, wished the young man good luck, and went down to the dining room for dinner alone. Though impatient to get away from the city, I reckoned another five more days would be needed, to get acclimatized, organize my sound equipment, buy supplies, and hire a moped before heading north.

When I finally reached the sanctuary of Barawa, I was overjoyed to find old friends and informants still eager to collaborate in the research I had begun before the war. My plan was to explore the extent to which the themes of traditional songs and stories found contemporary expression in the rap, reggae, dancehall, Afropop, bubu, gumbe, and grime music that had flourished in the postwar period. My formal proposal had been "that youthful rebellion against gerontocratic and patrimonial regimes, experimentation with drugs and altered consciousness, exuberant celebrations of life, and quests for social mobility, are variations on traditional preoccupations—tensions among kin and in-laws, resistance to authority, the longing for love, and the pain of separation and loss." The truth was, however, that this academic agenda was a pretext for returning to the remote village where I had, in the past, found inspiration and nourishment.

As for the war, I quickly realized that no one wanted to talk about it, despite Barawa having been twice overrun by rebels. It was as if the daily effort to produce food precluded any thought of revenge or even the possibility of prolonged grief. Within a few days I had followed the villagers' example, and the past scarcely entered my thoughts.

Undoubtedly, my sense of disconnectedness was exacerbated by being beyond the reach of cell phones, and my reluctance to travel two days on foot to Masingbi where a small and unreliable Internet café enabled me to assure my wife that I was in good health and to cash the moneygrams she sent me. But, after four weeks in the field, my staples of coffee, lentils, cooking oil, and curry paste—items unprocurable, even in Masingbi—were running low, and I had to return to Freetown to replenish them.

At the Institute for African Studies I casually asked if anyone had heard from Tom Lannon. No one had. In fact, no one seemed to know who I was talking about, even when I described "that tall white guy from England who was going to Kono." It was as though Tom Lannon had disappeared from the face of the earth. Perhaps he'd found the going too rough and returned to England. But then, having experienced this young man's need to project an air of independence, I was not only certain that Lannon was still in the country; I was sure the Englishman's failure to keep in touch with the institute was deliberate.

Determined to make the most of my limited time in Freetown, I completed my business within three days, returned to Barawa, and once again forgot about Tom Lannon.

After two months in the field, I found myself spending more time missing my wife than doing my research, and the tedium, heat, and isolation of the village were wearing me down. For hours on end I would sit on the porch of my host's house in a state of torpor, and the incessant demands on my time and resources by adoptive kinsmen were making me irritable and unforthcoming. None of these experiences was entirely new to me. But in the past they had always been offset by the relaxation of village life and the exhilaration I found in fieldwork. Rather than fall into a state of funk, I therefore decided to head south to Freetown and begin my planned interviews with musicians there.

Back at Fourah Bay College, I again asked if anyone knew what had become of the student from Cambridge. It wasn't that I wanted to see him, but for some reason—possibly because I remembered my younger self in this self-absorbed Englishman—I needed to assure myself that Tom Lannon was all right.

When I drew blank after blank, I decided to make inquiries at the British High Commission, which I passed every afternoon on my way to Lumley Beach for a swim.

The High Commission had no record of a Thomas Lannon. This was no cause for alarm, a consular officer assured me. Not every British citizen in Sierra Leone registered with the High Commission, and, unless I had evidence of something amiss, the consulate would make a note of my concern, together with my name and contact address in Freetown. "For the time being," the consulate officer said, "there's nothing more we can do."

My bungalow was shaded by locust trees, surrounded by rain-stained granite boulders, and overlooked the smoke-obscured slums and alleyways of the East End far below. At night I sat out on the verandah recording the sonic landscape around me—the throb of drums and hubbub of traffic in congested streets and then, like an inexplicable splash interrupting the sound of a river in the night, an irascible car horn or snatch of Afropop from a downtown bar.

Five days after my visit to the British High Commission, I dropped into the African Studies Center to collect my mail. A note in my pigeonhole instructed me to contact the High Commission "at my earliest convenience."

"When did you receive this message?" I asked the Krio receptionist, who was languidly lacquering her long fingernails.

With a show of utter disdain, she glanced at the memo and said she'd no idea.

I knew better than to press the point. I took the note, went downstairs, unlocked my moped, and rode to Spur Road. I was convinced the message concerned Tom Lannon. It couldn't be about anything else. And I feared the worst.

Within minutes of entering the High Commission, I was ushered into the presence of two consular officers who immediately asked to see my passport and explain my business in Sierra Leone and my relationship with Thomas Lannon. When I took umbrage at the interrogation, the senior official apologized for his brusqueness. Lannon had been detained by the Sierra Leonean security police several weeks ago and was presently languishing in Pademba Road Prison. Arrangements had been made for his release, but they were conditional on some individual—above reproach in the eyes of both the British and Sierra Leonean authorities—undertaking to care for Mr. Lannon, who seemed to be suffering from several as yet undiagnosed illnesses. This individual would also see that Mr. Lannon left the country within three weeks from the date of his discharge from police custody.

"What on earth is he suspected of doing?"

"Well, that's the other reason why we had to give you the third degree. He was arrested on suspicion of diamond smuggling. Since you were our only known link to him, we had to make sure you were not in this business together."

"How do you know I'm not?"

"I think your credentials speak for themselves, Professor Jackson. Again, we must apologize for losing our sangfroid and treating you so tactlessly. It's asking a lot. I'm sure you have far more pressing things to do than take care of this young man. But you did show concern for him. And it seemed only logical to us that we should turn to you. Will you help?"

I said I would. And instantly regretted it.

The room is filled with uniformed police and prison officials, all talking over each other. The consular officer who interviewed Tom Lannon two days ago is trying to get a word in edgeways.

Lannon's face is sallow and drained. The guard who brought him into the room suddenly retreats into the corridor and springs to attention, his hand quivering against his forehead in a tense salute. His eyes show no glimmer of recognition.

Lannon begs for a chair so that he can sit down.

There is an electric desk fan blowing papers about. The palaver goes on. The consular officer nods at me reassuringly. Then Lannon topples from the chair. When he is helped to his feet, I notice that his lip is bleeding.

The black Mercedes moves slowly through the thronged late afternoon streets. Lannon is sitting beside me in the back seat. He touches a forefinger to his lip, then inspects the smear of blood.

"There won't be any formal deportation order," says the consular officer, glancing back, "but they're going to require you to leave the country within twenty-one days."

"What day is it today?"

"Tuesday the fourth," I tell him.

"We will book you on the British Caledonia flight for Friday the twenty-first," the consular officer says.

Traffic comes to a standstill. Women in gaudy boubous, with basins of cassava leaf and dried fish on their heads, shuffle past the car. A street kid runs up and presses a copy of *Time* against the driver's window. The consular officer looks straight ahead with practiced immunity.

"Air conditioning cool enough?" he asks.

Tom Lannon is clearly exhausted, yet also seems euphoric. I follow his gaze. The roadside stalls made of wooden poles and sheets of iron . . . cheap Taiwanese underwear hanging from the rafters, polyester and cotton business suits, flip-flops and plastic sandals strung like onions, T-shirts and bolts of cloth printed with the president's dour face. People pour past in an endless stream, the teeming life of the city that went on uninterrupted during the days and nights Lannon lay like a sick dog in his cell . . .

We are moving again. The Mercedes accelerates smoothly and powerfully as we turn on to the road to Mount Aureol. There are clumps of bougainvillea among the dark green foliage. Kids hurl stones up into a mango tree . . .

When we reach the bungalow, I help Lannon from the car, guiding him toward the front verandah.

"You've taken quite a pasting, young man. Let's say you have a bath, change into some fresh clothes—I think I can find something that'll fit you—then we'll give you a decent meal."

Lannon resents my patronage. Weak as he is, he refuses to be a victim of charity, cajoled by the promise of creature comforts. In prison he dreamed of a hot bath, a shave, clean clothes, cotton sheets, but now he feels he is betraying or reneging on a vow. He wants to sit on one of the stones. Perhaps he does not want to forget the darkness and terror. Not yet. Perhaps he wants to find his own way back into the world. To collect his thoughts. To be wholly alive to the remains of the day.

But I am getting impatient and insist we go inside. Night will fall soon. I have the impression that we are in a painting by the Douanier Rousseau. There are clouds in the sky like gull's wings. I hold the screen door open.

"What should I call you?" Lannon asks peevishly.

"Whatever you feel comfortable with. I imagine you're used to some degree of formality at Cambridge. You can call me Professor Jackson or Michael."

"Michael Jackson!"

"Yes, the connection's been pointed out to me before."

Lannon peers at his ravaged face in the shaving mirror. Persona non grata, the consular officer called him. Lannon tells me that when he was a boy he thought it was Latin for ingratitude. I watch as he begins scraping gingerly at his beard with a disposable razor. His face is like a death mask. He dabs at the scabs with disinfectant and picks away wafers of dead skin.

When he is done, he fills a tumbler with water and gulps down the chloroquin tablets and rubbery capsules of Amoxil.

As Lannon lowers himself into the steaming bath, I leave the room to pour myself a gin and tonic. I can hear the young man in the bathroom, sighing with pleasure.

Minutes later I am summoned. Lannon has been scrubbing at the engrained dirt around his ankles and feet, and discovered lumps under his toes that are painful to touch. I see a screaming child in Barawa, held tight in its mother's arms while she digs the chigoes out of the soles of its feet with a sliver of raffia cane. When I tell Lannon what they are, Lannon is overcome with revulsion.

I find a sewing needle in my first aid kit, disinfect it, and observe Lannon's trepidation as he begins picking at the first lump. Gagging, he watches as the dead white calloused flesh opens, and pus and eggs ooze out . . .

I have prepared rice and dal. My guest has little appetite for what resembles a cow pat on a heap of maggots, but does not want to give offense.

"This diamond smuggling business?" I ask. "Is there any truth in it?"

"It's a long story," Lannon replies. And then abruptly, "Do you mind if I make a call on your cell phone?"

"Help yourself," I say, tugging the device from my pants pocket and setting it down on the table.

I have no intention of eavesdropping, but when Lannon goes outside to make his call, I cannot help but overhear almost every word.

"Cosmega?"

—

"It's me, Tom."

—

"I'm here, in Freetown."

—

"I can't.

—

"I can't. There's nothing either of us can do about it. We have to get on with our own lives."

In the morning, over coffee, I suggest that the young man owes me an explanation. "If I have to chaperone you for the next fortnight, I'd like to know who or what I'm dealing with. Does that sound reasonable?"

"It might help me," Lannon says, "to go over things. To get things straight in my own mind. If I bore you, just say so. I'll shut up. But I'd like to talk. To set the record straight, as it were. If it's all the same to you."

## Tom Lannon's Story

A little over a year ago, I attended a conference at the School of Oriental and African Studies in London where I met a young Sierra Leonean called Ezekiel Mansaray. When I asked if he was there to give a paper, he laughed. He'd been looking for a friend who was a student at SOAS; he'd simply wandered in to the conference out of curiosity.

I couldn't work out from his accent where exactly he was from.

"Are you working in London?" I asked.

"I'm a doorman."

"What does a doorman do?"

"He open doors for people."

"Like at a club?"

"Yes, like at a club."

I was both mystified and drawn to this wiry, black-bearded man who spoke slowly and self-consciously, as if the English language, or the English, were a minefield, and I admit I was slightly amused by the Burberry shirt, red tie, and cowboy boots he was wearing. When I asked him to join me for coffee, Ezekiel said he would not take a coffee, but would like to talk. Only much later did I learn that Ezekiel Mansaray never bought anything in a café or restaurant on the grounds that it was a waste of money.

I was surprised how well spoken he was, and how well read. He not only knew of Conrad's *Heart of Darkness*; he knew of Chinua Achebe's critique of Conrad, and thought Achebe was wrong to see Conrad solely as a creature of his times. "It is in wrestling with our circumstances that great writing is born, and Conrad wrestled with his as passionately as anyone."

I warmed to this man, and asked him if he, by any chance, was a writer.

"I try," he said.

I explained that I had a train to catch. "Are you sure you won't have something to eat? A cup of coffee? Tea?"

Ezekiel raised his palm as if in benediction. "I would like to ask a favor of you. I would like you to read something I have written. To give me an opinion of it."

"What is it? A story? A novel?"

"A novel."

"You realize, of course, that I am in no position to . . ."

"I am not asking you to pull strings on my account. I would value your opinion, that's all. You are obviously a literary man. It would mean a great deal to me to have your opinion."

"What is it called, your novel?"

"The Gates."

"Gates?"

"You will understand the image when you read it. It will not be strange to you."

From a battered plastic shopping bag, Ezekiel extracted a ream of dog-eared pages, held together with two rubber bands. I took the manuscript, placed it in my briefcase, and promised I would look at it. Then, after making sure I had his address and cell phone number, I rushed out into the street with Ezekiel dogging my heels. He apologized for having detained me. He expressed the hope that time spent reading his work would not be time wasted.

As I climbed into my taxi, leaving Ezekiel Mansaray on the pavement with his empty shopping bag, I felt as if this stranger had placed his life in my hands.

Ahead of me on the platform, a middle-aged man in a parka was helping a blind man onto the train. I followed them into the coach, the blind man taking the window seat, the other man cramming his rucksack into the overhead rack before taking a seat opposite him. As the train pulled out, this restive individual bent over, grabbed an empty bottle that was rolling around on the floor, and stashed it in the trash bin. He then asked the black girl with braided hair who was sitting in the window seat beside him if she would mind if he closed the window. The Good Samaritan, I thought. Busy with giving. The kind of person who would sacrifice his life to save a stranger. I glanced at the passengers across the aisle. A man about my own age was reading the score of *Lucia de Lamamoor* and holding a sharpened pencil in his right hand as if about to make an annotation or correction. This is his world, I thought. I looked at the black girl with braided hair. She was laboriously peeling the label off a bottle of Heinz ketchup. I watched her for several minutes, amazed at the concentration she brought to her task, and wondered what on earth she was thinking. It was only when she began reading the fine print on the label that I realized it was a lottery of some sort that required the contestant to transcribe some details from the label on the front of the ketchup bottle to the label on the back. Again, she did this with complete concentration, as if her life depended on it. I glanced back at the young man and his opera score. He was having difficulty concentrating. Two women opposite him were discussing an operation that a mutual friend had undergone at Middlesex Hospital. I transferred my briefcase from the seat beside me to my lap, took out Ezekiel's battered manuscript, and began to read.

For as long as I can remember our elders spoke of paths. Of roads that would help us prosper. Of rivers that ran clear. Our teachers told us that education would open doors for us. It would assure us of a future. And so I dreamed of being a doctor and of saving lives or of becoming an engineer who would bring light to our village. But we left school only to find that the roads were barred to us. There was no work. We had gone as far as we could go. We were strangers at the gate, waiting for crumbs, worse off than had we followed our fathers' advice and farmed. But there was no going back. We had glimpsed the road beyond the barriers. We had come to the open sea. And so we turned to our diviners. They laid out their stones. The gates were closed, they said. We would have to make a sacrifice to open the roads so that benefits would accrue to us. We did what we were told, but it made no difference. On the lintel of my father's house was a miniature gate, made of raffia, and a dirt-encrusted bottle containing a dark liquid that I imagined, as a child, to be a djinn. My father explained that these things kept witches away. They kept the doorway clear. They made the inside safe. Each farming season he would build a fence around his farm to keep out marauding animals. On a platform high above the ripening grain, my brothers and I would use our slingshots against scavenging birds. But my father had closed himself off from the world this way. He received strangers grudgingly. Not a day went by that he did not upbraid me for wasting my time attending school. And after war came down the road and our village was destroyed, he asked me what I now thought of the open road. But, in the end, I followed that road, accursed as it was. I sought to pass through the gate, as a camel passes through the eye of a needle. I walked the street of pain.

I was still reading when my train jolted to a halt at Cambridge. I walked to Johns in a daze and spent the rest of the day jotting down notes for Ezekiel about how he might improve his manuscript.

Over the next few weeks, Ezekiel phoned me every few days, thanking me for my encouragement, assuring me he would begin making the revisions I suggested as soon as he was more settled. I could never get a clear picture of his circumstances, but it appeared that he had lost his doorman job and was sleeping in a vacant office space where a friend was night watchman. When I expressed concern, he assured me that he was all right. He had "contacts"; he was "in transition"; there was a "new opening" on the horizon. He was used to being a ghost, he said, and he knew his way around the gray economy better than he knew how to negotiate the labyrinth of English life. I told him he was very welcome to stay with me in Cambridge if this would help, but he would not hear of it. I had gone out of my way already, reading his manuscript, helping him improve it; he would be ashamed to ask anything more of me. I was not assured. I was reminded of his refusal to accept my offer of a coffee on the afternoon we first met. And so I insisted, each time we spoke on the phone, that if he was in dire straits he should not hesitate to come to Cambridge and avail himself of my hospitality.

When he finally came, bringing with him what he called his "wordly goods"—two suitcases containing more books and papers than clothing—my gratification at helping Ezekiel with his writing was only increased by our growing friendship. Ezekiel spent long hours revising his manuscript, sometimes along lines I had suggested, sometimes taking the narrative in astonishingly new directions, oneiric, fantastic, violent, poetic, and making me marvel at the resources, experiences, and imagery he had at his disposal. If he ventured out, it was "to stretch his legs and clear his head," as he put it, walking for hours along the Cam or to outlying towns like Madingly, Trumpington, or Coton. Once or twice a week he would prepare Sierra Leonean dishes that my girlfriend Petra and I soon learned to relish. I was grateful for his presence. He mediated my ambivalent relationship with Petra with laughter and recounted anecdotes from his years of struggle in London. But of what befell him in Sierra Leone during the war he said nothing. Nor of his family. Nor of how he came to Britain. His novel was full of dark allusions to these things, but it was almost entirely based on his struggle to survive in London. The long hours he spent in the British Library, completing his education. His efforts to transform his thick West African accent, to disguise his origins, to pass through doors that had been slammed in his face, to be recognized as an equal by people for whom he was as insignificant as a stone. I could see that Petra's heart went out to him, not with pity but with a kind of angry compassion, and she would rail against the system that shut Ezekiel out, as though this might compensate in some way for the indifference of those who had made his life so difficult. As for Ezekiel, he no long deferred to me as a mentor and challenged my views on almost everything. He could not, for example, countenance the term *postcolonial*. His argument was that Africa was probably more under the baleful influence of the West than it had ever been, that Development and Aid were euphemisms for political blackmail, and smokescreens for European self-interest—dumping our trash on Africa's doorstep while calling it a gift, denying African countries access to Western markets while leaving them no alternative but to go into debt buying the commodities we produced. "You still exploit and marginalize us!" Ezekiel exclaimed. "You use us to make yourselves feel better about yourselves. You still need to think of yourselves as superior beings."

Toward the end of Michaelmas, I invited Ezekiel to give a seminar in my department. I thought his views should be heard and his novel read.

I regretted my decision immediately. None of my fellow doctoral students deigned even to glance at the two chapters that I'd photocopied and circulated beforehand. And I later rued having asked a man of Ezekiel's intelligence to explain, in terms an academic would understand, the arcane divinatory symbolism of his novel. After the seminar, strolling back to Johns, I apologized for my insensitivity at putting him in such an invidious situation. He smiled. "Thomas," he said (he refused to abbreviate my name), "it is you to whom apologies are due, for as your guest I failed to honor the trust you placed in me. As for your colleagues, they also owe you an apology for treating our friendship so casually."

A few days after this fiasco, Ezekiel packed his bags and announced he was returning to London. His decision had nothing to do with the seminar, he said. He had simply outstayed his welcome. When I suggested that he at least finish "The Gates" before he left, he said there were more pressing things in his life than his novel. It was time for him to go home, to return to "the land of my birth."

"But your book could well earn you an advance and pay your fare," I said.

"I have my fare," Ezekiel said.

The following morning, I accompanied Ezekiel to the station. I begged him to keep in touch. "You have my address," Ezekiel said. "But rather than write, why don't you come and visit me."

After the usual awkward pleasantries, in the course of which I urged him to complete his novel and allow me to find a publisher for it, he climbed aboard the train, pulled the door shut, and with that uncanny ability to disappear into himself that had disconcerted me many times before, he placed his bag on the overhead rack and settled into his seat, as blind to my lingering presence on the platform as he was to the other travelers in his compartment.

I walked back to my rooms in a dismal mood. I stared out at the turrets of New Court Gate and the backs, the chestnuts losing their rusty leaves, gray sky lowering. Mournfully, I surveyed the study my friends envied for its spaciousness, its tranquillity, its view. On the walls I had hung a tapa cloth from Tonga, a framed photograph of a Samburu girl from Kenya, a priceless mudcloth from Mali—intimations of worlds I had never visited. It depressed me to realize that my world was, in effect, this one cluttered room. The cloisters through which I walked each morning, the Bridge of Sighs, the cobbled courtyards, the porters with whom I exchanged small talk and from whom I received my mail. How odd to think of Ezekiel doing the same job for so many years. Had he too worn a uniform? That ridiculous livery of the doormen you see outside London clubs and hotels? Or had he been more like the doorman in Kafka's *Trial* who kept the poor countryman forever from the Law? Swiveling in my chair, I contemplated the stacks of papers, piles of books, open files . . . reminders that I still had not settled on a research project or a place where I might pursue it. Again I turned to the window to gaze into the bleak day, yielding to my mood of nameless loss.

When Ezekeiel's postcards began to arrive from Sierra Leone, I did not mention them to Petra, presuming they would neither interest her nor draw us together. In any case, what could I say that might explain my depressed spirits, my sense of isolation, when I could not even explain these things to myself? At High Table, I found myself bored by the academic chitchat and could not curb my impatience for dinner to come to an end. At seminars I would inexplicably lose my train of thought, become irrationally irritated by the questions and answers flying to and fro around me, and want to flee the room as if it were on fire. I took long walks, sometimes alone, sometimes with Petra. "You seem very preoccupied," Petra said. "I am thinking about Ezekiel," I said, using him as my alibi. "Oh, and how *is* Ezekiel," she asked, in a tone that suggested she might have become jealous of our friendship. "Do you ever hear from him?" I did not respond. I didn't want her to point out yet again how oddly I was behaving.

But later that day, I suddenly knew what I wanted to do and the title of the thesis I would write was clearly in my mind. "Hearts of Darkness: Nineteenth-Century Narratives of the West African Hinterland." I did not confide to Petra my plans for going to Sierra Leone, but shared them with my closest Cambridge friend.

We met in The Lion. It was late morning, and the pub reeked of stale beer and Jeyes Fluid. Harry and I took a table near the fireplace and raised our glasses to "good times and bad." But before our glasses had been set down on the table I was pressing Harry for an answer to my question: "Have you ever asked yourself, what if the life you're living isn't your true life, the life you were meant to lead, but some kind of false trail you'd stumbled down and simply become used to? That you are little more than a creature of habit? Have you ever experienced this?"

Harry fetched a theatrical sigh. "The thought has crossed my mind. But then I tell myself, what else would I do? I am reasonably . . ."

"Perhaps you have found your path."

"And you haven't found yours?"

"I think I have. And it's the same path young men like us stumbled down a hundred years ago."

"This isn't about you and Petra, is it?"

"No. Yes. I mean, the problem isn't Petra. It's me."

"You haven't fallen for someone else, have you? One of those American girls you tutor?"

"Jesus, Harry."

"What then?"

"You remember Ezekiel Mansaray?" I said.

"That West African chap you had staying with you? The one that gave that seminar on his novel?"

"'The Gates.' Yes. He's back in Sierra Leone now . . ."

"Now the war's over?"

"I don't know if that's the reason. But he's gone, and I've been think-ing about his book. This idea of gates opening and closing. Opportunities missed or not seen or simply nonexistent. I thought it was metaphysical. A kind of Tutuela-like imagining of a parallel universe. But now I see clearly that Ezekiel's talking about the real world, the world he lives in, the world you and I live in. I couldn't see it before. I've academicized everything. Now I want to see that world for myself, to risk myself in it. Not view it from the safety of a hotel or an air-conditioned car. How can I pretend to understand the literature that is coming out of these countries if I have no first-hand knowledge of them?"

"Well, I haven't lived in the nineteenth century, and that hasn't prevented me from having something interesting to say about Eliot and Dickens."

"But, don't you see, I have the option! That's the difference! I am *free* to enter Ezekiel's world. I *can* know it from the inside."

"Sort of what if I were an African?"

"Come on, Harry, you can do better than that."

"I'm afraid I can't, Tom. You've lost me. You say you don't want to be metaphysical, yet what is all this idle speculation and vain conjecture if it isn't metaphysical? I'm sorry, but I don't know what you're going on about. I really don't."

"I've already spoken to Mainwaring," I said. "I'm going to Sierra Leone."

"The white man's grave!"

"And Cambridge, I suppose, isn't?"

"To each his own, Tom. But speaking selfishly, I will miss you. Cambridge will be, as the good Donne said, the lesse."

When I went to Thomas Cook's to buy an airline ticket to Freetown, the girl at the counter asked me why I wanted to go to Sierra Leone, as if I wasn't in my right mind.

The following day I told Petra what I had decided. I would retrace Alexander Gordon Laing's steps from the Sierra Leone coast to the interior and write a book that juxtaposed his experiences in 1822 with my own experiences 180 years later. Petra closed her eyes for a moment, and then, as if she had prepared for this very contingency, she said, "You must do whatever you feel you must, Tom, and I . . . I will keep the home fires burning, I suppose."

I hated myself for not confessing my other reasons for going to West Africa. But I wasn't exactly sure what they were myself. And I was grateful that Petra should neither question my motives nor argue against my going. Taking a step toward her, I kissed her on the cheek. I felt like Judas.

On the day I left for London, Petra walked me to the station.

It was only when the train was drawing in that she broke the silence. "Please phone me when you arrive, to tell me you are all right."

"There may be no phone."

"You know what I mean, Tom."

"I will do my best."

"You've changed, Tom. Perhaps we have both changed. Perhaps that's it. And we hadn't realized."

When I did not reply, she said, "My God, I feel as if I'm saying good-bye to you forever."


## Cosmega

On the flight to Freetown I found myself increasingly anxious about the status of my relationship with Ezekiel and whether I was, as Harry Eckersley had put it, "in thrall to the idea of destiny," traveling to Sierra Leone without having established Ezekiel's exact whereabouts or whether he could accommodate me. But I had his work address and assumed it would be fairly straightforward to run him to earth.

At Lungi Airport fragments from a Malcolm Lowry story drifted through my head . . . *that inenarrable, inconceivably desolate sense of having no right to be where you are . . . of something slipping through the hands of your mind, as it were, and that, seen without seeing, you can make nothing of . . . while behind you, thousands of miles away, it is as if you can hear your own real life plunging to its doom . . .*

UN helicopters, like gigantic and ghostly cicadas, sat on the tarmac. Remotely, in the gathering haze, lay the tattered palms and massed greenery of Africa. As I moved listlessly toward the crowded Arrivals Hall and Immigration Control, raucous shouts and outraged cries broke over me in waves. A disgruntled officer stamped my passport without a word. Young men besieged me, vying to carry my bag, to find me a taxi, or help me change my sterling into leones. Then I was swept away in a maelstrom of clamoring, agitated black people, like the pathetic individual I had seen several nights ago on TV, borne down a flooded street in some South American town, ignominious and hapless in the muddy torrent before being washed down a storm water drain.

On the ferry I inhaled the warm, briny air off the river. I was captivated by the inexplicable eddies and ripples that occasionally disturbed the sluggish stream. And I looked inland, to where the great river vanished in a green confusion of mangroves and mist, feeling sick in my stomach at the prospect of trying to find my way through that hinterland and at my harebrained plan to retrace Laing's steps. I bought some oranges from a young woman who was diligently peeling the thin green rind and stacking the fruit on a tin tray. She wrapped the money I gave her in the corner of a cotton cloth she wore around her waist, knotting it securely . . .

As the Bullom shore dwindled in the haze, the rusted roofs of the city and its immense cotton trees materialized at the foot of the range, and a nearby group of young English men and women began talking excitedly about their return from furlough. I assumed they were working for an NGO and thought them excessively self-conscious, as if onstage, projecting an image of seasoned sojourners. Yet I envied them. They knew where they were going.

That first night, drifting off to sleep in the ill-starred Majestic Hotel, I had the curious impression that I had journeyed, not through space but through time. I could not believe that this room in which I found myself, with its rain-stained, sagging ceiling panels, its defunct air conditioner and broken chair, coexisted with the college room in which I had sat, only twenty hours ago, gazing out at the lifeless trees in the softly falling snow. I thought: now, at this very moment, Petra will be falling asleep in her room at Newnham. But then I told myself, no, this cannot be true. She exists not elsewhere, but in the past. She has already passed out of my life. She exists only in past time. And then I thought of Ezekiel, who I would surely find tomorrow. He did not exist either. He will exist tomorrow, when I find him. Petra is past. Ezekiel is future. I am present. Like the reggae I can hear in the street, the honking of gridlocked traffic, shouts from the alley, footsteps in the next room, the smell of mildew and urine . . .

In the morning, after searching in vain for a café or restaurant, I bought some fried seedcakes from a street hawker and made my way to an address in Garrison Street where the hotel desk clerk told me I would be able to e-mail or telephone England. The street was lined on one side with bookstalls—dog-eared and anomalous volumes such as *General Thoracic Surgery*, *Business Mathematics*, and *The Flowers of Evil* (Mills and Boon, not Baudelaire) cheek by jowl with ballpoint pens and miscellaneous stationery. Among the books I came upon a folded tourist map of Sierra Leone. An auspicious find, I thought; a sign that I was on the right road. On the other side of the street was a row of makeshift booths draped with secondhand clothing. I had been told to look out for the shoe market, and, sure enough, there it was—a section of the street filled with fake designer runners, cheap imports from China, secondhand brogues from God knows where, women's high heels, men's loafers and work boots, and glossy black patent leather footwear for the would-be businessman. A flight of grimy concrete steps led to international services. In a gloomy, curtained room, I paid a sullen woman the fee to open a Yahoo account. But no sooner had I begun writing my e-mail to Petra than the power failed. The young woman explained that I should come back later. "I'll try again tomorrow," I said, without conviction, and asked if she could tell me how I could find my way to Broadcasting House.

After returning to the main street and locating the newly renovated law courts where workers were cementing metal railing into place, I turned left at the cotton tree and set off up Pademba Road. Along the scuffed edge of a deep streetside drain, I fell into step with scores of others, barefoot, toting head loads or sauntering along with small wooden trays of razors, ballpoint pens, trinkets, cheap watches, and cosmetics. After passing the prison, I came to a roundabout and was within sight of the place where Ezekiel worked. I was pleased with my accomplishment. I had not got lost. Everything was working out. Here was the special court cellblock where those charged with war crimes were being held. And here, opposite, was the Sierra Leone Broadcasting Service.

Outside the ramshackle, double-story building, two young men with amputated arms begged me for a dash. But one look at their unsightly stumps, where blunt machetes had chopped through their elbows, was as much as I could take. I stumbled into the shadows of the building, unable to find the words to even explain that I had no money, no change.

There was a large room off the first landing filled with editing tables and sound equipment. Along the corridor was another room, with spot lamps, tripods, and black backcloths—presumably a recording studio. I asked the young woman who was leaning against the doorjamb if she could tell me where I might find Ezekiel Mansaray. She nodded toward the first room I had passed. Retracing my steps to the editing room, I found another smaller room that led off it and a group of men and women sitting in front of a blackboard taking notes. I stood in the doorway, coughed, and asked if anyone knew where I might find Ezekiel Mansaray.

"He no dae," a woman said conclusively, turning in her chair. Then, switching to English, she added, "His wife was here a minute ago. Why don't you take a seat and wait?"

I was confused. I knew Ezekiel had a family, but this side of his life had somehow never registered with me. I had seen him as a loner, an exile, his life defined by his writing.

I sat at the back of the room and tried to make myself unobtrusive by picking up a local newspaper (little more than a broadsheet really) that lay on the chair next to me.

The Imam of Ibadul Mosque in King Jimmy, Sheikh Ibrahim Koroma has strongly condemned terrorism and violence. "Terrorism and violence must be mercilessly crushed," he said. Addressing Muslim youths, Sheikh Ibrahim Koroma declared that "Islam forbids hijacking airplanes, ships and other means of transport, and has forbidden all acts that undermine security." The King Jimmy Sheikh warned Muslims not to go astray, saying, "God says that the penalty of those who fight God and his prophet and spread violence and terror is death by crucifixion or have their hands and legs chopped off." Raising the question of why Islam is branded by some as the religion of terror, Sheikh Koroma said, "You must know Islam's firm stance against all these terrible crimes that are attributed to it."

Forgetting for a moment where I was, I was on the verge of laughing out loud, smugly savoring the prospect of sending this clipping to Harry, when a vivacious woman, her black hair meticulously braided and beaded, entered the room and was directed toward me.

"Kushe," she said warily.

"Mrs. Mansaray? Mrs. Ezekiel Mansaray?"

"Well, that is not my name. But you are looking for Ezekiel, nottaso?"

I explained that I had flown in from London yesterday and, yes, I was trying to find Ezekiel.

The woman was now looking at me with undisguised suspicion. Yet her frown and pout did not disguise the mind-numbing beauty of her face, the cheekbones like polished wood, the sculptured mouth.

"Did you write to him," she asked, "to say you were coming?"

Without waiting for my reply, she informed me that Ezekiel had gone up-country to attend his uncle's funeral. She had no idea how long he would be gone.

"Is there any way I can contact him?"

"I have no idea."

Again we were at loggerheads.

"What did you say your name was?" she asked.

After telling her, she appeared to soften a little, and said she was Cosmega. "Ezekiel tells me next to nothing about his acquaintances," she said. "Here or in England. I am sorry, but that is how it is."

"He didn't exactly tell me much about his life here either," I said. "I did not even know he was married. But I can see you are in a meeting, so I won't keep you."

As I turned to go, she asked where she could find me."

"I'm at the Majestic Hotel."

"Why are you staying at the Majestic?"

"A taxi driver recommended it."

"You should not be staying there. You should be in one of the tourist hotels. They have been renovated since the war. There you would be comfortable."

"I was hoping to avoid tourist hotels," I said.

"Are you with an NGO? Are you here on business?"

"I'm a student. From Cambridge University. I'm studying the contemporary West African novel. That's how I came to know Ezekiel. Through his writing."

"You study Ezekiel?" And she looked at me quizzically, expressing amused disbelief.

"Does that sound so odd?"

She laughed. "My goodness, I had no idea he was famous!"

"I don't know about famous. But much admired, yes. At least by people who recognize exceptional writing."

"And you've come all this way just to see Ezekiel?"

"I'm afraid so, yes."

"Why didn't he ask you to stay with him?"

"I didn't write. I came on the off chance."

"Eh! You came all the way to Sierra Leone on the off chance?"

She made the phrase sound ridiculous, and I was beginning to feel extremely foolish and very tired. It was as though the Ezekiel I had known in Cambridge and the Ezekiel his so-called wife was scornfully referring to were very different people.

"If you are Ezekiel's friend, you should be staying with us!"

"I wouldn't want to impose—"

"This is Africa, Mr. Lannon. It isn't imposing. You are our stranger, our guest."

Minutes later, we were climbing into her battered VW beetle and heading back into the city.

"It's not far, you'll see," she said. "We'll pick up your things at the Majestic, then I will take you to our house on Signal Hill. You must be tired and hungry after your long journey."

That afternoon, after a meal of rice and fish, which I ate alone, I slept solidly for an hour, waking in the cool of the evening to the shouts of children and Cosmega calling them in Krio to come eat. I joined them in the parlor. The kids had homework to do, Cosmega explained. But she wanted them first to satisfy their curiosity about the white stranger. If they didn't get a good look at me and ask me all the questions they wanted to ask, they would neither eat their dinner nor do their homework nor sleep.

Later, when the children had gone to their rooms, I sat with Cosmega in the parlor. It was now my turn to satisfy my curiosity.

"When Ezekiel came to England, you stayed on in Sierra Leone?" I asked.

"The children and I stayed, yes. Ezekiel had to go. He would have been killed if he had stayed."

"It must have been hard for you."

Cosmega smiled. "*Life* is hard," she said. "Being separated from my husband is not."

Ezekiel's marriage to this stunning but intimidating woman was the last thing I wanted to talk about, so I turned the conversation to the war, asking Cosmega if she had been in Freetown in January 1999, when the rebels overran the city.

"We ran away," Cosmega said with a self-deprecating laugh. "When Johnny Paul Koroma came out of prison and made his coup, I knew we would not be safe. We had videos in the SLBS archives, evidence of his crimes. And it was clear from the very beginning that he had cut a deal with the rebels. I took the children and drove to Lumley Beach. Some British marines helped us onto a boat. We went to Banjul. We were among the lucky ones."

"Have you always worked in journalism?"

"Not at all. This is Ezekiel's job. I took it over when he went to England."

In the days that followed I spent most of my time at the house, writing in my journal, helping the kids with their homework, talking to Cosmega, or simply sitting on the balcony and gazing out over the city, the lines of traffic crawling toward the cotton tree, the antlike trails of people in the narrow streets, the smoke from cooking fires, the haze-obscured sea. One morning I braved the downtown traffic, but at Garrison Street the power was down again and the generator wasn't working. I tried to make a phone call, but there was no reply, either from Petra's college or mine. I was relieved. Until I had found some justification for being in this godforsaken place, or could clarify my own motives for coming, it seemed pointless to talk to her. But, rather than afflict her with further uncertainty about my state of mind or what I was doing, I located the post office, bought a postcard, and scribbled a few lines assuring her that I would write at length when I was more settled. Having mailed it, I changed some money in the bank—which took the best (or should I say, worst?) part of an hour—then walked back to Signal Hill via Congo Cross. This took another hour, the perspiration soaking through my shirt and the cloying air making it difficult to breathe.

In the lane outside the house, I found Ibrahim and Jeneba wending their way back from school. They were bashing at the mimosa bushes alongside a concrete wall. "Go sleep, go sleep, go sleep," they chanted. And as they whacked, the small leaves blenched and curled, the whole bush darkening as they closed. "Tie you lapa, you man dae kam, tie you lapa, you man dae kam," they cried in the same singsong voice. I asked them to teach me the words and to tell me some useful Krio phrases. They laughed and obliged.

In the yard, Ansumana was draping clothes over the bushes to dry. Ansumana was a distant kinsman, who worked for Cosmega in exchange for a place to sleep—a small concrete pillbox in the back yard.

"Missus dae?" I asked.

"She dae."

The children burst into laughter.

That evening, as I was eating, again alone, Cosmega told me that two small children had been killed not far from Broadcasting House when they unearthed a grenade with their hoe and it exploded under them. Two other children were in Connaught Hospital. "The little girl has lost both her legs," Cosmega said, "and her brother is having his right leg and arm amputated tonight."

I instantly remembered the stream that wound down from the hills, women tending their small plots of spinach, lettuce, and cassava, and could not reconcile this pastoral image with the tragedy Cosmega had just described.

My bewilderment must have been evident, for Cosmega asked if I would be interested in accompanying her on an assignment the following day. She was driving to Waterloo to visit a refugee camp. I was welcome to come along.

And so I saw for the first time the misery of what it was to live in limbo, to live what one woman described as a "bush life," because, as Cosmega explained, it was lived outside the pale of normal human society where people worked, built houses, made farms, and raised children . . .

"Believe me," Cosmega said, as I dogged her heels through the fetid alleyways of the camp, "the worst of it here is not from the trauma of war. It is not the things that Western journalists come looking for. It's the things the war has brought in its wake, like AIDS. It's the endemic scourges of Saralon. Things we have suffered here for centuries. Malaria. Childhood dysentery. Maternal mortality. VVF."

"VVF?" I queried.

"Vesico-vaginal fistula. Its what happens when girls become pregnant before their bodies are fully developed. The fetus is often too large to enter the birth canal. It compresses the bladder against the sidewall of the pelvis. To make matters worse, midwives sometimes try to expel the baby by pushing down hard on the girl's belly. The baby dies. Tissue dies in the girl's bladder, creating a hole through which urine leaks continually. The girl is condemned to lifelong incontinence."

I shuddered at the thought.

"You see. You jump to the conclusion that the girl is repugnant and unclean. That she will be shunned. Driven to live like a leper alone in the bush. This happens. But it rarely leads to the breakup of a marriage. This is what Westerners cannot understand. That we learn to live with adversities that you could not endure."

"Is there any cure for the condition?"

"I don't want to oppress you with these things, Thomas Lannon. But this is how things are here. This is what we live with, war or no war."

Driving back to the West End, often at a standstill in the narrow, congested streets, I found myself oppressed by what I had seen and heard. The girls that Cosmega had described to me, leaking urine. Others who had been raped and used as sex slaves by the Revolutionary United Front, now breaking stones. And then the young men who had crowded around me, begging for a dash, hissing to get my attention, who were without work and had no hope of regaining the livelihoods they had lost. "What can be done?" I asked Cosmega. "Is there nothing one can do?"

"Money," Cosmega said. "It's simple as that. Money to go home, if they have a home to go back to. Money for grain to make their farms. To start a small business. To renew a driver's license. To pay school fees. To pay for minor surgery. It costs only $180 to repair the damage from fistula. Money to marry. Money, or the kind of work that will enable them to earn it. It's the same for everyone here, to some extent. Even me. By local standards I'm well off. I get about $100 a month, and unlike some government offices, SLBS usually pays its journalists on time. But almost everything I earn goes on rent and the children's school expenses. Sometimes I cannot afford to pay for electricity. Not that you get your money's worth, what with the power cuts and everything. And, with petrol prices going up, I don't know how long I can afford to drive. If it wasn't for my sister in Bonthe, who sends us rice and dried fish, I don't know how we'd get by. During the war we learned to expect nothing. Now it's over we expect things to be different. Perhaps we expect too much."

"Doesn't Ezekiel . . . ?"

"I will not live on dead money."

"Dead?"

"It comes from diamonds. It would destroy us, just as it destroyed this country. It's the money of death. The money of shit. Like the money that whores are given. The money from theft. I would not risk the life of my children by bringing it into this house."

At first I did not mind being alone with Cosmega in the evenings, but I had begun to feel uneasy about the way she hurried the children off to bed and was so curt with them when they called from their room. One night, after grudgingly responding to their calls, she returned to the parlor in bare feet, wearing a new dress and smelling of perfume. Unnerved by this, I began to spend my afternoons in aimless research at Fourah Bay College and my evenings in the Guest House bar. I had brought photocopies of Laing's *Travels* with me from England and now, with the aid of my tourist map, I tried to identify the explorer's route from the mouth of the Sierra Leone River to the far north. At first I failed to find any of the place-names he mentioned, but then I got lucky. Rosar, on the Rokel, still existed. Further east: Nonkoba, and Mayoso. Less easy to trace was Laing's route after leaving Mabum, though I identified the villages of Kania and Yara in the eastern foothills of the Sula Mountains and from there could guess his probable route to Falaba. But, according to my map, bush tracks, not roads, connected these remote villages, and I simply could not imagine myself alone in that wilderness, ill-equipped and, I now realized, unmotivated. Besides, hadn't Cosmega impressed upon me the dangers of venturing up-country?

It was as though I was under a spell, immobilized and imprisoned in Cosmega's house. The next night, when I mumbled something about going to my room to read and made to leave, she asked if her company bored me.

"No, no . . ." I stammered, "I usually read for a while before I go to sleep."

"Is that what your wife does too?"

"I am not married."

"Your girlfriend, then?"

"Yes," I said, tentatively.

"Do you read the same books?"

"Sometimes," I said.

"What are reading now?"

"It's called *Chronicle of a Death Foretold*," I said.

"Why do you want to read about death? Why don't you read about life?"

"It's not just about death," I said.

I saw I would have to stay now. I said: "I don't have to read, you know."

"Are you sure?"

"No, we can talk."

"Will you be able to get to sleep without reading?"

I did know whether she was being facetious or not. Her face was perfectly composed, and she was beautiful. I was afraid of her. I was afraid of her frankness and of my feelings toward her. Would she excuse herself tonight only to return to the parlor wearing another gown, another perfume?

But she fetched a thermos of tea and sat on the sofa away from me and apologized for talking about things that were none of her business.

"I wasn't offended," I said.

"You are in love," Cosmega said. "I shouldn't pry."

She seemed as determined to abject herself as I was determined to set her mind at ease, and it was only when she poured the tea that it became possible to steer our conversation in another direction.

"Do you think you will hear from Ezekiel soon?" I asked.

"I doubt it. He comes and goes in his own time. He is often away."

"The children must miss him when he's not here."

"I think it is a relief," she said. "You must understand, ours is a marriage in name only."

"But you are still together?"

"In the eyes of the children, yes. In the eyes of God, perhaps." A shadow seemed to pass from her face, and she paused. "You know, Thomas, it was the women who suffered most in this war. Far more than the men. You would not believe the terrible things that women suffered. And yet it is always the women who endure. We are the stronger ones. We plant the gardens. We bear and raise the children. We trade. We keep the home fires burning."

This uncanny echo of Petra's remark on the eve of my departure for West Africa unsettled me. I gazed out into the night where bats were massing and squealing in the mango trees. And then I asked Cosmega if it would be possible for me to find Ezekiel if I went up-country. If she could tell me how to find him.

"It's possible," she said. "But, just as I told you, it's not safe in the north these days."

"Isn't that just Ezekiel's justification for keeping you in Freetown?"

"You must be careful wherever you are. You don't know who you can trust. I don't think you can possibly understand what happened here over the last ten years. You should wait for Ezekiel to get back. It would be safer. And you could help me, if you wanted. You could help me with some of my stories. You might even get them into the English papers. Help get the word out, help us tell the world what happened here and how we are struggling."

"I would like to help," I said. "But I really do want to see Ezekiel. And, besides, I can't go on imposing upon your hospitality indefinitely."

"That's the kind of thing an Englishman would say."

"But I am an Englishman," I said.

# Sangbamba

It took me two days to get to Ezekiel's village in the far north. I endured the first day crammed into a beat-up poda-poda, unable to understand a word of the boisterous talk around me, and cursing myself for having set out so unprepared—with only a bottle of mineral water, a handful of tea bags, a jar of instant coffee, and a small cache of personal medicines. I wondered if my fellow passengers saw me as incongruous as I saw myself—Clarence in *The Radiance of the King*. Yet, as the day wore on, the goodwill with which people tutored me in Krio, shared their food, and took an interest in where I was going put paid to the paranoid reflections that were beginning to take hold of me, and as our vehicle banged and lurched into the interior my disorientation gave way to a kind of fatalistic contentment. I had only the haziest sense of where we were. I had left Freetown precipitously, not even waiting for confirmation that Ezekiel had received the message Cosmega had entrusted to a cousin of hers who was going up-country. And my initial reaction to the Sierra Leonean hinterland had been one of complete bewilderment—the clustered thatched huts, bundles of firewood and bags of charcoal stacked along the roadsides, people sitting in the shade of a mango tree or walking down a dirt path into the fastness of an oil palm plantation. There were moments when I felt so vulnerable that it was a struggle to breathe. Cosmega had opened a door to me, and I had backed away. Why? Because I had lost all sense of what was true and right? Or was it simply that I did not have the guts or commitment to enter the world she said she could open up to me? When I discovered that she could have sent a message to Ezekiel at any time and had chosen not to, I felt cheated and angry. It gave me an excuse for leaving and obliged her to make good on her promise to let Ezekiel know I was in the country. But what if I had stupidly misread the signs and she had been neither flirting with me nor trying to turn my affections away from her faithless husband?

Every few miles along the eroded highway, we ground to a halt and the driver or his sidekick poured water from a Texaco can into the gurgling radiator. Or else we were stopped at one of the UN checkpoints where blue-helmeted, melancholy soldiers sat behind sandbags or manned makeshift barriers—reminders of how recently death and disaster had come down these same roads.

It was late in the day when we reached Alikalia. A battered, rusty sign on the roadside told me so. An air of desolation and ruin hung over the place, intensified by the dying daylight—boarded-up shops, piles of rubbish everywhere, some of it smoldering, and the upturned carcasses of gutted vehicles. It fitted my inner mood. And as I crawled from the poda-poda and attempted to stand upright in the dusty street, I felt I had done my dash and had every justification to turn tail, retrace my steps to Freetown, and take the first flight back to England.

With Ezekiel nowhere in sight, I began to panic. After standing haplessly in the street for several minutes, I made my way along a row of burned-out stores and found refuge in a shabby bar—a fly-specked Star Beer calendar on the wall and two torn vinyl chairs beside a tin table. The owner was wearing a white net singlet that scarcely contained his enormous belly, and when I asked if I could buy a drink he simply nodded toward a wooden crate of beer and Fanta near the doorway.

The owner's eyelids closed over his rheumy eyes as he uncapped the bottle I handed him. When I slid a 20,000 leone note across the wooden counter, he seemed so burdened by the transaction that I gathered up the dirty, crumpled notes he gave me as change without a word and went to the doorway to drink my soda and ponder my next move.

An overladen poda-poda was jolting and swaying down the street, negotiating potholes. It pulled up by a derelict-looking Shell pump where there was a long line of jerricans and plastic containers on the concrete slab.

The street was shadowless. I heard women's voices in the market, the blood coursing inside my head, the driver of the vehicle shouting across the street. But I did not immediately notice the men in dark glasses standing under the colonnade a few yards away.

It was difficult to know if they were watching me, but their faces were fixed in my direction, and when I looked around I realized there was no one else who could have been the object of their gaze. I drew back into the bar, gulped a mouthful of Fanta, and slipped the empty bottle back into the crate. When I turned, they were standing over me, silhouettes against the glare of the street, the black pools of their artificial eyes filled with the fragmented reflections of my own face, the stacked crates of beer, and the wall calendar. They were uniformly dressed in denims and high-heeled cowboy boots, with jet shirts unbuttoned to the chest, disclosing hammered name tags on cheap gold chains. One had a sheathed knife strapped to his calf. There was something disconcertingly feminine about them.

"Wusai yu di komot?" demanded the one with the knife. He was now close enough for me to smell the perfumed soap he used and see his lacquered fingernails.

"Freetown," I said. "Why?"

"You cross the border, nottoso?"

I supposed he meant the border with Guinea to the east.

"That's in the other direction," I said.

"You no dae cross the border?"

"I came up from Freetown," I repeated.

"No."

He cleared his throat and spat. The gobbet of spit rolled in the dust like a drop of mercury.

"What do you mean no?"

"You Franci?"

I didn't know whether he was suggesting I was a Franciscan or demanding to know if I was French.

"I'm from England," I said.

"You American?"

"No, I'm English."

"Waittin na yu name?"

When I told him, he jammed a matchstick between his teeth and ruminated.

"Waittin?" he said, screwing up his face as if my words had caused him pain. Then he jabbed a lacquered fingernail at my wallet and demanded to know what was in it.

I opened the wallet and showed him my Visa card, my Heffers card, and the tatty banknotes the barman had just given me.

"Wusai yu passport?"

I said I didn't have my passport with me.

He gestured at the notebook in my shirt pocket.

I pulled it out and waved it in front of his face. He grabbed it, and tried to read what was written in it, but his shades obviously made the task difficult. Or else my handwriting was illegible. Or else he couldn't read.

He passed my notebook to his sidekick who tilted it first one way then the other, as if this might help him decipher my scrawl. The first man spat his matchstick onto the ground and, with an air of contemptuous disappointment, said, "No American?"

"That's right," I said.

The man with my notebook sneered, then let it slip through his fingers to the floor. "No American," he said, mimicking his alter.

Then they were gone.

I asked the barman for a beer. He gave no indication of having been dismayed or even having witnessed what had just occurred. With an unsteady hand, I prized off the beer cap. The readiness with which I'd answered their sinister questions angered me. My hand was shaking as I lifted the bottle to my lips. I needed a cigarette. I hadn't smoked for years, but now I was asking for a packet of Lucky Strike, tearing it open, and realizing I didn't have a light.

I walked out into the hammering heat of the afternoon, my head filled with smart answers to the ridiculous questions I'd been asked. I was sick to the stomach that I had let them intimidate me, that I had let them see my fear.

In the market, women sat immobile in the shadows beside basins of rice. In a concrete cubicle, swarming with flies, a man in ragged shorts hacked at a shredded fat-streaked carcass with a machete.

As I trudged back up the street, I thought I heard my name being called. And, suddenly, there he was, and my despair was gone.

"This is unbelievable!" Ezekiel exclaimed. "I can't believe my eyes! But you didn't let me know! Why didn't you warn me? I would have come to Freetown to meet you. Tom, this calls for jubilation! I can't believe you made this journey. All this way to see me, Cosmega said. All the way from England just to see me!"

As he rattled on in this vein, I was smiling. Not only in relief that he had received Cosmega's message, but in self-congratulation that I had run the risk of not finding him and been rewarded for my faith.

"I see you've got rid of your beard," I observed. Clean-shaven, he looked leaner and more careworn.

"It suited me in England, but not here," he said, seizing my bag and urging me to follow him.

We walked past some ruined buildings, their concrete facades pock-marked with shrapnel and bearing the faded signs of their erstwhile owners—Khoury and Sons, Choitrams, Hassan Masoud. Then we picked our way down a lane, where gray water dribbled and pooled among the garbage, and came out on the edge of a field to a solitary cow, surrounded by white egrets, nosing the rice stubble.

"We will spend the night at my cousin's house," Ezekiel said, "whereupon we will set out for Sangbamba in the morning. That is where I was born. I will show you everything. You will meet my family. We are all honored that you are here."

I think it was Ezekiel's 'whereupon'—a reminder of the archaisms with which he liked to pepper his speech, telltale signs of the self-educated man—that made me feel for the first time since leaving Cambridge that I was on the right path.

We made the journey to Sangbamba on Ezekiel's moped, bumping and scraping along a worn laterite path that wound interminably through tall brakes of elephant grass and over insignificant streams. It was as much as I could do to cling to him. My eyes were closed against the dust. I breathed through the grubby handkerchief I had tied across my face and prayed we would reach the village before the sun burned me to a frazzle.

"You won't need anything," Ezekiel had assured me. "My brother's house has everything you will require. A good bed. A mosquito net. Privacy. You've got your antimalarials and water purifying tablets. If there's anything else you need, we can send to Freetown for it. Do not vex yourself. You will be in good hands."

Ezekiel's brother's house surprised me. Standing in the middle of the village, it seemed, at first sight, to be the only building that had escaped the auto-da-fé of 1998 to which Ezekiel had alluded that morning when warning me, with uncharacteristic understatement, that Sangbamba still bore the scars of war.

Bala was sitting behind a treadle sewing machine at one end of the porch. A huge man, bearing no resemblance to his diminutive brother, he sprang to his feet like a djinn released from a bottle, grasped my hand, grinned, and said I was most welcome. After a few perfunctory remarks to his brother, Ezekiel ushered me into the parlor of the house where a self-effacing young woman was sweeping red dust and debris from under the long coffee table in the center of the room. "Come," Ezekiel said. "This will be your room. Bala's wives will fetch hot water for your bath. You have only to ask, and they will bring what you need. Remember, you only have to ask."

I had not dared think of what I might find in the north. Certainly I had not expected this sanctuary. A bed with a foam mattress, a cotton tablecloth for a sheet, a nylon mosquito net that had seen better days, yet would still protect me, and a bedside table where Ezekiel suggested I could write my letters home.

"But you are surely tired," Ezekiel said. "I will let you rest. When you are ready we can eat."

I had to admit that I was both famished and thirsty. If it was possible, I would like to eat right away.

In fact, two covered enamel dishes had already been placed on the table in the parlor, and as we sat down opposite each other Ezekiel enjoined me to eat my fill. "You can use the spoon," he said, as if he hoped I would decline the option, "or you can eat like me, with your fingers."

Ezekiel then called for water to wash our hands.

I tried to imitate the way he spilled water from the enamel mug onto the palm of his hand and rubbed his fingers together before shaking them dry over the cement floor. But in the end I had to use both hands, even though I knew the left should never come into contact with food.

Hungry as I was, I chewed the gristly pieces of beef and swallowed the parboiled rice without appetite. My mind was swarming with questions I could not bring myself to ask—about his marriage, where he was actually living, whether he was working on a book, and what Cosmega had implied about his money coming from diamonds. And, as Bala's youngest wife, Mantene, shuffled in and out of the parlor, first with a mug of drinking water, then with two hard-boiled eggs, "a gift for the whiteman," I wanted to ask Ezekiel how she had lost her arm. But the war, like everything else that day, was beyond my grasp, beyond my power to put into words.

Despite my dumbness, Ezekiel did volunteer one piece of information as we sat that evening on the porch at Bala's house: he was investigating the

RUF's transformation into a political party. He wanted to know whether it was possible for the boys who had taken up arms and lived in the bush for so many years to reenter civil society. Whether they would be accepted back and under what conditions. "Many of them are here amongst us," he said gravely. "You will meet them. The very ones who helped destroy this village . . ."

But I was no longer listening. I was thinking of the young men who had accosted me in Alikalia and wondering what they had done during the war.

At first light, mist streamed through the barred window of my room. I lay on my back, hands behind my head, looking up at the rafters and the tin roof. A rooster crowed. There were voices in the lane and then the grating sound of a metal bucket being set down outside my door. When I peered out, the parlor was empty. I carried the pail of hot water out into the backyard, where a half-circle of elephant grass mats protected the latrine from prying eyes. The latrine itself was a deep hole, surrounded by a small cemented area where one squatted to shit. The stench from the hole was nauseating. But I told myself I would get used to it. I *had* to get used to it. I refused to allow any longing for home comforts to drive me from this place.

I stripped naked and stood on the uneven patch of concrete, dashing water over my shoulders and scrubbing every inch of my scrawny body. The body of a scholar, I thought. I felt exposed and grotesque. I wished I was black. I wished there was some way I could blend in with the surroundings and disappear from my own gaze.

I ate breakfast on the front porch with Bala ensconced a few feet away, an aluminum kettle in one hand and a safety razor in the other with which he was cautiously raking his chin and jowls.

He called out gruffly to Mantene, who scurried off through the house. A few minutes later, she returned with a thermos of boiled water.

"Waitin yu na de drink?" Bala asked.

I was not sure if he was volunteering to make a drink for the two of us or politely inquiring what I preferred to drink. After some hesitation I took the thermos, which Mantene had set down beside me, and made two mugs of instant coffee. As I made to pass one to Bala, he laughed. "I de pray now," he said. "No coffee."

After unrolling a small raffia mat, Bala commenced his prayers, kneeling in obeisance to the east, oblivious to all else.

I felt like an interloper, and it was a relief when Ezekiel joined me with a packet of cabin bread, a bunch of bananas, and some oranges. Ignoring his brother at prayer, he asked me how I had slept and proposed that he teach me the local patois for greeting people in the morning. There were different phrases for the afternoon and evening, he said, but these I could learn later.

As Ezekiel sipped the coffee I had made for his brother, I brought myself to ask about Mantene and how she had lost her hand.

"Alas," he said, "she was one of us who was in the wrong place at the wrong time. She and her daughter both."

I was stunned.

"Is her daughter here?" I asked.

"She was taken to the United States," Ezekiel said. "She has never returned."

"How so?"

"Because in war terrible things happen, my friend. And when wars are over even worse things can happen. Don't ask me how so."

I asked about his writing. Apart from his research, had he yet finished "The Gates"?

"It has become the journey," he said, leaving it unclear as to whether this was the title or an allusion to the trials and tribulations of the writing process.

"I am at an impasse," he said. "It is too much about myself. I need to find ways of making it more allegorical, whereby it becomes the story of our times and not just my own."

When I asked him what journey he had in mind, Ezekiel sighed. "There was a time," he began, "when I could not wait to get away from this place. My family was suffocating me with their demands. I was in a marriage I had not desired. And my obligations to my in-laws were as pointless as they were onerous. I was twenty-five, and the world was beyond my grasp. I wanted to be a man, but not a man like my father. Not a farmer, but a man of knowledge. A man of the world."

As Ezekiel drank his coffee, I followed his gaze out into the mist-swathed village where people were standing huddled around small fires, blankets pulled about their shoulders.

"I received a minimal education from the mission school in Alikalia," Ezekiel said. "Father Joseph told us that education would give us freedom. It would be a portal to a brighter future, a guarantee of fulfillment and work. But it gave us nothing except a prejudice against farming, a disenchantment with our fathers' way of life, and the bitterness of broken dreams. And so I came back to Sangbamba, married, made a farm, and revised my dreams. But there was nothing for me here, or so I thought. And I left again, as a spirit leaves a corpse. Dead to myself. Dead to this world. I went back to Alikalia for a while and worked for a Lebanese store owner there. But I soon got fed up with being at his beck and call. Fetching and carrying. Bearing the brunt of his frustrations and abuse. Little more than a slave. So I went to Sefadu and joined Bala in the diamond fields. It was not my scene either. I had no ambition to strike it rich. I wanted to broaden my horizons. I wanted something other than a big house, a car. I wanted a better life, though I could not say what that might be like. And so I moved to Freetown. Lived with our cousin Lansana. Hung out in the streets. Sold newspapers. That's how I got into journalism and began to write. That's where I learned my trade. But then the *Courier* offices were destroyed by government thugs, a gagging order placed on everyone who had worked there, and I was adrift again. Then came the war."

"The war," I repeated, as if the subject was not mine to broach.

"Yes, the war," Ezekiel said bitterly. "But, after the first rebel assault on Barawa, I escaped. Crossed the border into Guinea. Made my way north. Hitching rides. Eking out the money Bala had entrusted to me. Walking for days on end. Sleeping in the bush. Begging hospitality from villagers in return for telling stories or playing the flute." Ezekiel laughed. "Busking, you might say. I reached Niamey, in Niger. There were hundreds of us there, waiting for money at the Western Union Office. Trying to find the means of paying for food and water and transport across the Sahara. I cabled Cosmega at Broadcasting House. She told me it was safe in Freetown, that I should come home. In Niamey I heard rumors of what we would encounter. People dying in the desert. Armed robbers stealing your money and leaving you to die. Guides abandoning you. I heard of a group of Sierra Leoneans, stranded in the middle of the desert when their lorry driver drove off during the night. When their water ran out, they collected their own urine in bottles, added sugar cubes, and drank it to slake their thirst. They hallucinated and walked off into the wastes, thinking they had seen palms or the roofs of houses. Only two survived. I began to have doubts. But I had reached the point of no return. My home was no more. And so I pushed on, using the money Bala gave me and the money Cosmega reluctantly sent. We traveled by day. At night we slept under the lorry. We ate bread and tinned sardines. We carried water in the inner tubes of car tires because they held more than bottles. I had terrible diarrhea, probably from polluted water. But I drank it just the same. At night we huddled under a tarpaulin, our only blanket, but could not sleep for the cold. But we made it to Tripoli. It took eight days. In all this time I had not washed. My body was covered in insect bites. We looked at one another and saw disheveled madmen. But this was only the beginning of our tribulations. We paid our way to a safe house along the coast where we waited for ten days. We feared the Libyan police, who were on the lookout for black Africans. One night, after paying an Egyptian middleman, we embarked on a fishing boat heading to Italy. The boat broke down many miles from our destination. The boatman tried to restart it many times. We also tried. But it was no use. Women began screaming that we were doomed. Some of the men began to pray. We drifted for ten days. When a ship appeared on the horizon, the Egyptian boatman dived overboard and started swimming toward it. He must have been crazy. Within minutes the sea had swallowed him up. People were losing consciousness. We had no water. No food. Some were drinking seawater and losing their minds. Flailing about, clutching their bellies, shouting the names of their loved ones. One man stepped over the side, thinking he was stepping onto a wharf. We were withering under the sun and freezing at night. As for me, I prepared to die. Our boat was found the following morning, our eleventh day at sea. Thirteen of us were dead in the boat. We had dumped many others overboard. Perhaps as many as forty. Some had drowned. Only ten of us survived. We were taken to Lampadusa. The medics gave us intravenous drips and medicines. They treated us well. But it was three weeks before I could leave the hospital. The authorities let me travel to Rome where I told my story at the British Consulate and was given permission to enter the United Kingdom as a refugee. That is the journey, Tom. That is what I am trying to describe.

"Not a journey to the promised land," I said.

"No, Tom. No streets paved with gold. No kindly merchant with a beautiful daughter. Not even a cat!"

"You have come a long way. And I don't mean geographically."

"I have achieved very little, Tom. I have read widely, to be sure. I taught myself to write in the tradition that you were raised to respect. I even wrote a book. But at the end of the day I was as disenchanted as ever. And I was filled with shame. You become your own worst enemy. A vehicle backs out of a driveway, the driver has not seen you, but you are convinced he is trying to run you down. Someone walks into you on the street, you apologize, but the other person ignores you and hastens away, as if you are carrying the plague. A book you ask for at the British Library isn't brought from the stacks for five hours. You ask, why the delay? Is it because no one believes that a scruffy black man can be a serious reader? You pass a withdrawal slip to a teller in the bank, and he suggests you sign with an X and expects you to share the joke. You suffer this growing conviction that you have no right to be there, no right even to exist. And all the while you are keeping up the pretense that you are about to be miraculously transformed. That your writing will make you accepted. I am not ungrateful, Tom. I owe a great deal to you. But sometimes we sink into such despair that our imaginations run away with us. We imagine that some natural justice will prevail, that we will be rewarded for everything we have endured. Or that some wealthy benefactor will take pity on us, like Magwitch with Pip.

"I remember, one time, I got a friend to take some photos of me standing in front of the Houses of Parliament and Big Ben. So I could send them back home, and show my family how well I had done. It was one thing to bear my own disappointment. It was another thing to bear the shame of disappointing my family. So you put on this brave face. You vow not to give in to the bitterness and hunger that gnaws at your soul. You decide to tough it out. To stay as long as it takes, to find the money to send home, to acquire the evidence, the proof, that your journey has been worthwhile. But when I look back at the humiliation and the loneliness and the hunger and the pain, and the doors slammed in my face, I know this is something that no human being should have to go through. To be at the mercy of one's dreams, to know they are false, but not be free to discard them. Perhaps that's why I cannot finish 'The Journey.' I did not finish it in reality. I failed to find what I was looking for. And I could not pretend."

That morning Ezekiel took me to meet the chief and elders of the village. "We should have done this yesterday," he explained. "It is important to pay our respects and explain why you are here."

And so I sat nervously on a metal folding chair, wondering how on earth I could explain my presence to these old men with somber faces, sitting on the porch of the chief's house in the heat of the day. But it was, Ezekiel assured me, imperative that one show one's goodwill by simply sitting with the elders for a while. And so, as he painstakingly translated the stock phrases with which every visitor is met, I sat like a child among strangers, alone, uncomprehending, and powerless. When we were done, and I had received a calabash of rice and a handful of kola nuts, Ezekiel suggested we stroll around the village so that everyone could greet me and see that I was his "stranger."

Apart from Bala's house, which the rebels had used as their headquarters, every other building had been stripped of its roofing iron and set on fire. With the mist now lifting, there was nothing to mask the fire-blackened mud walls of ruined houses and the saplings, grass, and creepers that were already reclaiming them for the bush.

Certainly there had been some rebuilding. The chief's house was new. Bundles of thatching grass were piled beside other new dwellings, and village women were smearing white clay on the mud brick walls. "Many people are still in the bush," Ezekiel said. "They are staying on their farms. But, now that the harvest is over, some will return. Others are still not convinced that the war is over."

"And you?" I asked. "What do you think?"

"We can always pretend," Ezekiel said, "but no, I do not think it is ever over."

If Ezekiel had seemed embittered and depressed, guiding me around the village or recounting the story of his journey to Europe, he was nothing short of ecstatic when he told me about his nephew Yandi, who he was teaching to read and write, and his niece, Sanfan Fina, whose initiation he was sponsoring.

I met her that afternoon. She was sitting on a stool in the shade of an orange tree near Bala's house, brushing and oiling her hair in preparation for braiding. She looked at me shyly as I approached and lowered her eyes as I asked her, through Ezekiel, how she felt about her imminent coming of age. She responded like an English child anticipating Christmas. She had looked forward to this day all her life. She would be dressed in the finest clothes. Her relatives would fuss over her, showering her with gifts. And at the end of it all she would be a woman, mature enough to marry, to bear children, to have a life of her own.

Her optimism was impossible to reconcile with what Cosmega had told me at the Waterloo camp about VVF, and I could only wonder whether Sanfan Fina was aware of the dangers ahead of her, or, if she did, whether it would make the slightest difference.

Over the next few evenings I saw her often, moving about with a small entourage of her age-mates, calling at the houses of relatives to dance and sing. They would come out of the darkness into the penumbra of our lanterns, wearing beaded skirts, hair braided and decorated with ivory combs and snail shells, clapping and singing to the unremitting drums.

*Soon the dancing will be over*
*Childhood will be over*
*And the dancing done . . .*

We watched them dance, leaning toward the drummers, arms undulating like the wings of birds. And we gave them money as they danced and sang of their prospective husbands, to whom several had been betrothed since infancy.

"It is the beginning of a new life for them," Ezekiel said. "They will soon die to their childhoods. And we, who have raised them, and brought them so far, will learn to live without them. Besides," he added, "this is the first initiation in Sangbamba since the war. For us, it is a sign that our community has come back to life."

But his tone of voice betrayed him, and I was moved to ask if he was thinking of Sanfan Fina.

"I was thinking of my daughter," he said.

"Jeneba?" I asked, since he had mentioned her to me once.

"No. This is the daughter of my first marriage. It was long ago."

"Where does she live now?"

"She is dead."

I reached out and touched his forearm. "I am sorry."

"It happens," Ezekiel said. "These things happen." And he muttered something about fire giving birth to ash, which I did not understand.

I did not want to press him further. But he began reminiscing about his own childhood, and I fell to listening again.

"I used to be afraid of everything. The djinn. The night. The shades of the dead. Had it not been for my uncle Morowa, I would never have mastered this fear. You will meet him. In those days he was master of the Dununma, one of the most powerful djinn. He told me that only by facing the things I most feared would I overcome my fear. It was like initiation, I suppose. I would have to die in order to live. Or like that journey to Europe and the years I wasted in that wilderness. It is the same in the stories we tell here. You go out into the wilderness on a journey in search of fame or fortune, but you cannot hope to succeed on your own. You need some magical medicines. You need the help of a djinn. But the catch is, the djinn asks you, in return, for the life of someone you love. You see, there are no real gifts in this world! We pay the price for everything we get. And some of us pay more dearly than others."

"You're not saying that your daughter died because you were successful."

"I'm saying that one cannot always divine the causes of things. Why things work out the way they do."

"You once told me that life is a struggle and that great writing is born of this struggle."

"Well, that's the kind of thing one says when one is not struggling! But we say here that one's destiny is under the influence of allies and opposites.

When I was a boy, an old storyteller called Denka Marah was my ally. So too was my uncle Morowa. You were my ally in Cambridge. But there are opposites and opponents too. It might be a stone that trips you up on the road, a bad marriage, a bout of illness, the death of someone you love. But even when life seems to be nothing but a struggle against opposites, and you have no ally, you can still preserve your honor. Even if you lose the struggle, you can be proud that you fought hard against everything that was set against you."

It was then that it occurred to me that Ezekiel's journey had roughly followed Laing's route from Tripoli, only in reverse, and that my own plan of retracing Laing's Sierra Leone journey to Falaba had, without my fore-knowledge, brought me accidentally to a village through which the Scots explorer must have passed on his way north from Yara. As I fell asleep, I pondered Laing's unconsummated marriage to the daughter of the British consul general in Tripoli, two days before he set out across the Sahara, and how he carried Emma Warrington's pallid cameo with him to Timbuktu, only to perish in the desert, murdered by jihadis, his papers burned for fear they possessed magical powers.

Every night, courtyards were lit by flickering lanterns. Shrouded figures filed past, urging us to confess ill will, to clear the air. If we did not mend our differences, the neophytes' wounds would not heal. In dusty compounds men placed their hands over bowls of white rice flour, and swore their grievances gone. Children owned up to petty misdemeanors. Wives admitted to real and imagined affairs. And, for a time, everyone took refuge in the belief that they could put the past behind them and that virtue would be rewarded with prosperity.

Meanwhile the masquerades went on. Children, dressed in their fathers' clothes, moved from house to house. Their bodies were daubed with charcoal and ocher, their faces hidden behind wads of raffia. They mimicked their parents and elders. One boy stood in front of me, scribbling furiously in the palm of his hand with a make-believe pen.

One morning, Ezekiel asked me if I would like to accompany him to a remote farm hamlet to consult a "soothsayer." His family had relied on him for advice for many years, and, since the date for Sanfan Fina's initiation had now been decided, it was imperative to find out what hidden dangers might lie along her path. "It is a perilous time," Ezekiel said. "We must do everything in our power to ensure that all goes well."

"What kind of perils?" I wanted to know.

"The ill will of a stranger, a witch in our midst, a knife in a shaky hand . . . there are many things. You never know. But Pa Bockari will bring to light what lies in the shadows."

And so, as the sun was breaking through the early morning mist, we set out.

For an hour or so we followed a rutted path through the grassland. There was no sound except for a bird, endlessly repeating its name — sulukuku, su-lukuku, sulukuku — and we seldom spoke. When we entered the forest, the sun was splintered or fell in dusty shafts from the high canopy. Butterflies sought pools of sunlight. Monkeys clambered noisily from one high flimsy branch to another. Strange birds shrieked overhead.

After an hour of stumbling over roots and rocks, we came to the clearing where Pa Bockari lived.

He was sitting in a hammock under the low thatched eaves of his house. Without moving, he returned Ezekiel's obligatory greetings with the familiar declarations of goodwill.

While Ezekiel quickly explained the reason for our visit, I eyed the array of fetishes attached to the lintel of the old man's front door. Mysterious bottles, stoppered with pieces of rag. Bundles of raffia sticks, bound with string. Tufts of cotton wool.

Bockari rose from his hammock and pushed open the rickety door behind him. After rummaging in a small storeroom, he emerged with a folded prayer mat and a monkey-skin bag. Once seated on the mat, he indicated that we should sit opposite him. Pa Bockari then spilled a score or more of river-polished stones onto the mat and raked through them with his long fingers. Then, gathering some of the pebbles in his hand, he began to chant, calling to the bush spirits who were his allies and eyes. As he murmured his cryptic phrases, he shut his eyes and gently rapped the back of his hand against the mat. Then he laid out the stones in ones, twos, and threes and examined the pattern.

Ezekiel quietly explained that the pattern would reveal a prognosis. To avert disaster or reinforce an auspicious prediction, a sacrifice would have to be made. This, Ezekiel said, was why Pa Bockari was now repeating the procedure.

As it turned out, Ezekiel had to sacrifice seven white kola nuts in water, three to be given to a woman, four to a man. Then a red goat had to be ritually killed at the end of Sanfan Fina's initiation to smooth her path into marriage.

Intrigued by what was unfolding before me, I asked Ezekiel if an outsider like myself could consult a diviner.

Ezekiel was clearly taken aback. Perhaps he assumed that a European would regard the entire business as chicanery and superstition. Perhaps it had not occurred to him that I might have unspoken troubles on my mind and need guidance. But, when he saw that I was in earnest, he asked Pa Bockari if it was possible to do what I had asked. The response was a bemused yes. And so I pulled some leones from my shirt pocket, handed them to the diviner, and had Ezekiel translate my questions for him. Was Petra all right? Was my absence causing anyone grief?

Perhaps I was obliquely asking Ezekiel. Needing to get my concerns into the light of day, to voice them, to get some distance from them.

Bockari repeated his procedures and told me, through Ezekiel, that there was no danger on my path and that my family was well. But I was enjoined to sacrifice a length of white cloth to a man I respected and carry a double-bladed knife with me at all times.

As we trekked back to Sangbamba, I asked Ezekiel to tell me more about the techniques we had just witnessed. Ezekiel said he did not know much about soothsaying. Only those with the gift of four eyes, or a djinn as ally, could see into the future, and indicate what ritual actions would secure prosperity or prevent misfortune.

"But you said Pa Bockari referred to some of the stones as doors or gates," I said.

"The world is crisscrossed with paths," Ezekiel replied. "The paths connect us with one another. But danger and death come down these paths, as well as life. And sometimes the paths become blocked. If there is ill will between neighbors, for example, or secrets and conspiracies. In the best of all possible worlds, the gates along these paths would be open. But sometimes we have to close them. To keep the dangers out. Just as farmers fence their farms against wild animals."

"So the diviner is a kind of gatekeeper between visible and invisible worlds?"

"You could say that."

I asked Ezekiel about the devices I had noticed on the lintel at Pa Bockari's house. Were these ways of sealing the house against evil trespass?

"Yes, it's the same idea," Ezekiel said wearily. "They protect the house against dangers from outside. They are like gates or locks. Same as the things people wear around their necks or sew into their clothing. They seal the borders. We call them *kandan li fannu*, protecting or enclosing things. You will see them everywhere."

That evening, sitting on the porch at Bala's house, as the sun melted into the haze of the harmattan and palm birds chattered and roistered nearby, I felt strangely calm. Such calm as to make me realize how agitated and distressed I had been since leaving England with my lame excuses and selfish dreams. I was in no doubt as to the status of Pa Bockari's comments. They were no more than educated guesses, intuitive stabs in the dark. And yet they had assuaged my misgivings and hardened my resolve. There was also the peace that came from being so far from anywhere, in a world without the trappings and distractions of modernity. Time out of mind. History in abeyance, despite the evidence of the cruel swath it had cut through this region. I felt, at times, that I was on a long-distance flight, lulled into a kind of lotus-induced torpor, released from the need to act, blissfully passive. But there was a difference. In Sangbamba it was as if I was seeing the world for the first time. Almost as if I had acquired a diviner's second sight. I saw everything as a child might. The palm birds in the clustered fronds, the bloodshot sun sinking into the hills. The thud and rasp of a mortar rhythmically falling into a wooden pestle. And the protesting howls of Mantene's infant son, whom she bathed every evening in a large calabash of cold water below the porch. And I thought of that line of Baudelaire's that Petra once loved to quote: *genius is innocence recaptured at will.* Except that I had willed nothing.

So one day flowed into another, and I lost track of time. I acquired a smattering of Krio. I wrote in my journal. I accompanied Ezekiel on his journeys to forest hamlets and neighboring villages to interview boys who had been abducted by, or voluntarily fought for, the RUF. And I met old Morowa, the master of the mysterious Dununma. He came to me one morning, complaining of sharp pains in his arm and shoulder. The reason was obvious; his right hand was swollen with septicemia. Among the few medicines I had brought with me from Cambridge was a supply of penicillin. I gave the old man two tablets and instructed him to swallow them with water, one immediately, another in the evening. Then, for a week, I went out of my way to find him twice a day and ensure that he continued the course to the end. To my great relief, the swelling subsided and his pain went away, leaving me to wonder whether he, for all his expertise in magical medicines, would see me now in a new light. Henderson the Rain King!

All this time the neophytes were sequestered in a bush house. There they would undergo clitoridectomies and remain for several weeks while their wounds healed and older women instructed them in the complexities of sex, the secrets of childbirth, and the ethics of womanhood. I tried to talk to Mantene about what was going on, begging an embarrassed Ezekiel to translate for me. "It is not for men to know or see," Mantene said. "But every girl must go through *biriye*. Except she dies, every girl must overcome her fear if she is to become a woman."

## Ezekiel's Story

It was against this background of the initiations, with its rumors of hidden menace and its intimations of rebirth, that Ezekiel gave me the dog-eared pages that chronicled the terrible events that had befallen him and his village toward the end of the dry season of 1995.

After finding a corner in the parlor of Bala's house where I could read undisturbed, Ezekiel left me. "I will be with Bala if you need me," he said. But I hardly heard him, engrossed as I was by the manuscript I now held in my hands.

It wasn't the first attack on Sangbamba. The RUF came eighteen months earlier, brandishing their weapons and pillaging. They were seeking revenge for the *tamaboro* attacks on them.

Mystified, I went out to the porch to seek clarification from Ezekiel. "Who were the *tamaboros*?" I asked.

Ezekiel explained that the tamaboros were a kind of militia, recruited mainly from among village hunters, who used their special powers of night vision, immunity to bullets, stealth, shape-shifting, and silence to track and ambush RUF brigades. Terrified by the supernatural abilities and guerrilla tactics of the tamaboros, the RUF retreated to their strongholds in the south. But the military junta in Freetown, itself increasingly threatened by the successes of the tamaboros, abruptly ordered the militias to disband. It was at this time that the RUF regrouped and, with the help of renegade soldiers, reclaimed the diamond fields and drove north in retaliative raids, scorching and burning at will. "But they targeted only certain houses, and certain people," Ezekiel said. "The destruction was by no means random. And Sangbamba survived, more or less unscathed."

I went back indoors and began reading again.

In those days you never knew what to expect. To travel anywhere was to risk ambush and death. And stories spread like wildfire, of atrocities committed by the RUF and South African mercenaries alike. Small boys tortured or thrown to their death from helicopters by the South Africans. Old men thrown into pit latrines and drowned or made to drink boiling palm oil. Fathers forced to rape their daughters. Everything was possible. You took nothing for granted. You did not know what to believe or who to trust. But, even if you believed everything you heard, you could do nothing. You could only go to ground like a hunted animal or sit at home like a frightened child, unable to tell the difference between the word *fire* and actual flames. And so I traveled to Alikalia that March, and on to Sangbamba. I met no rebels. I heard of nothing untoward. And, like others, I let myself be lulled into a sense of false security.

The very day I returned here, Chief Keli called a meeting. The news from Freetown was that the Nigerian ECOMOG forces had forced the junta from power and that President Tejan Kabbah had returned to

Freetown from Guinea where he had been living in exile. Junta soldiers and their RUF allies were now fighting a last-ditch battle against superior forces. They knew it was only a matter of time before they were defeated. And they were filled with hatred for the people that had supported the president.

I remember Chief Keli conjuring the specter of another epoch, when the horsemen of the Maninka warlord Samori invaded our country, looting and sacking the main towns where, for many years afterward, piles of skulls marked the abandoned settlements. The elders here were divided in their opinion as to what they might do. Some muttered against the RUF and of the years of misrule that had brought them into being. Some argued that in the event of a rebel attack they could easily flee the village and take refuge in the bush. Some were outraged at the very idea and argued that the RUF was a spent force and would not venture so far north. Fear of the tamaboros would keep them away.

It was the time of the initiations, a time of foreboding. Though we celebrated the beginning of new life, we lived in constant fear that life as we had known it was about to end. You could not escape the fear. It weighed on your mind. Every visitor to the village was subject to suspicion. Was he an RUF spy? A renegade soldier pretending to be one of us? Did he have reliable news of what was happening in Freetown? Could we rely on the Nigerians and the Guineans to protect us in the event of an attack?

One morning I was at Bala's house. We were all on edge. Only the women seemed immune to the rumors. They had formed a long line. Heads held high, expressionless faces daubed with white clay, they moved as one, swaying from the hips, flexing their arms, moving a pace forward, a pace to the side, advancing across the courtyard as though with hoes across a hillside, tilling the earth.

As they moved, they sang. And their voices were possessed of a stately and haughty power.

I was standing in the doorway. My nephews, troubled by the profound and urgent unison of the women's voices, fidgeted behind me. "Come back inside," they begged. "You should not be seen."

The women were taunting us with cryptic songs:

*The tree that withstood fire*
*has been felled by white ants.*

*The lordly hawk, high in its tree,*
*descends to the earth for food.*

Then time slowed down.

It was like rain, when it suddenly stops.

Everything I heard and saw was vivid and prolonged, as though I was watching myself watching, hearing myself hearing—the RUF boys bursting into the compound, the women's deadpan faces as they danced row upon row, seeming not to see.

"What's happening, what's happening!"

The voices behind me were frightened but far away so that by the time I realized it was me of whom an answer was demanded it was too late and I said nothing, though I had no words anyway, all words buried now in the silted depths as I watched the wall of the women's bodies blocking the path of the armed thugs, the rhythm of their chant unbroken.

When the firing began, it seemed again that everything was in slow motion. Grass flew up from the thatched rooftops in puffs of gray dust. A mud wall was ripped by a line of bullets.

Abruptly, the gunfire ceased.

I was in a state of shock. There was a buzzing and ringing in my ears. My hands were shaking. I heard firing from another part of the village.

Then I looked down at the terrible theater unfolding in the courtyard, the RUF boys shouting now, shouting for the women to stop.

"Cunts! Cockroaches! Cock suckers!! Where are your men!"

But the entranced movement of the women, not fearful, not even incredulous, but void of recognition, made it seem as if the drug-crazed boys before them were a mirage.

*Stop, why don't they stop?* My head ached as I willed them to stop.

The sun blazed in the sky, pulsating in time to my own blood. I could smell the sweaty fetor of the room behind me.

Then Bala was whispering desperately in my ear. "Come, we can get out the back way!"

I could not move. I was transfixed by an indigo and orange gecko that had scuttled onto the porch steps at my feet. Its head rocked hypnotically. Its body swayed. In the courtyard the women were still moving in a line, still singing. I recognized snatches of the song. The women had composed it in support of the president. But now they sang it with a shrill and nerve-wracking intensity, heads thrown back, eyes half-closed, flaunting their disdain for the men who barred their way.

I watched aghast as they shuffled forward. Aluminum anklets gently clashed. The beadwork around their hips and wrists and necks clicked and whispered like insects in the hot grass.

Mal koinya
*a load may bend our backs*
*but nothing can break our will,*
mal koinya,
*when people move together*
*no one can come to harm . . .*

Their audacity and courage stupified me.

"Shut up! Shut up! We will shoot!"

The RUF boys were backing away from the women. Their eyes were wild and scared. One boy shouted, "Get the captain!" Others hoisted their weapons and stabbed the air. This "captain," I would soon enough discover, was Musa Evangeli, who had attended the same school as me in Alikalia.

Defiantly the women danced, their voices strident and taunting.

"Cunts!" one of the RUF boys screamed. "Fucking cunts!" And still screaming, he opened fire.

Others did the same. Burst after burst of gunfire. The women only yards away. Hands going up. Bodies crumpling like emptied sacks.

And then a terrible silence . . . nothing . . . until a fading, piercing, ringing sound filled the void, as if the sound of the gunfire, the shrilling of the women, and the RUF boy's demented cry had fused and were drifting away with the blue smoke.

I felt very cold. The RUF boys, their fury spent, surprised by their own devastation, shrank back. In the courtyard, several women groped about or lay lifeless in the dust. One woman sat slack-jawed, shuddering. Another had clapped her hands across her ears, though the courtyard was now deathly quiet.

A long time seemed to pass before any of the women comprehended what had happened or those who had been hit felt any pain. But, with the first horrified scream, a clamor of keening and outraged cries filled the courtyard.

A small strangled cry was forced from my throat. Then I hurtled down the steps.

The bullets had hit low. Several women were sitting, staring with stricken faces at burning wounds in their thighs. One woman writhed and choked in agony, clutching at her belly. Dark crimson blood oozed between her fingers. I felt nauseous and weak.

Then I saw Sinkari, Bala's senior wife. A bullet had smashed her foot. She was biting her lip, struggling not to cry out. One hand gripped her lower shin. With the other she was trying to wipe the kaolin from her face. Where was Bala, though? He must have run for it.

As I knelt beside Sinkari, I became aware of other men moving around me. Suddenly Yandi, my nephew, was there too, his face ashen, looking at me with bulging eyes.

I glanced toward the RUF boys. Some were watching us in vacant astonishment or contempt. Others were retreating under a hail of blows and screams of abuse from several old women.

"Go inside. Get all the cloth you can. Clothing. Anything!"

Yandi did not budge.

"Go!" I cried.

As he staggered away, I tore off my T-shirt and crawled over to the woman behind Sinkari. The lapa around her lower abdomen was saturated with blood. Where the kaolin had flaked from her forehead, the skin was dry and scaly like wood. She observed me with a kind of dimmed awareness that seemed already to have carried her beyond pain, beyond that place. As I tried to staunch the bleeding, she gestured feebly and I took my hand away. I realized I could do nothing for her.

"Be brave," I whispered hoarsely, "be brave." But it was not her that needed to be calmed.

Suddenly, Musa Evangeli's boys were all around us. Haranguing us. Saying they would kill us all. Shouting at us to evacuate the courtyard.

I went on preparing bandages, helping the women dress their sisters' wounds. Flies were crawling everywhere. Children were crying. The air was rent by screams.

"Lef, lef, lef!" the thugs shouted over me.

"Fuck off!" I screamed. "Fuck off!"

My eyes were burning with tears of rage.

"Lef em!"

The muzzle of an AK-47 was rammed into my kidneys, and I was forced to my feet.

One glance back was all I managed before I was driven off. Yandi was nowhere to be seen.

We were herded into the chief's compound.

The entire village seemed to be there, massed under the mango trees. The air was filled with dust and the stench of bodies. Children were whimpering in the crush. Two men were balling each other out, as if, I thought at the time, their vehemence would somehow save them. A woman was crying, "Evil is upon us. The world has come to an end."

As though enclosed by an invisible barrier, we struggled to compress ourselves even further, anxious to hide ourselves, to evade recognition, to be shielded against the next onslaught.

There were RUF boys all around the compound, blocking the lanes. Some were dressed weirdly in what looked like women's wigs. Some wore shades and dreadlocks. Some had bandoliers draped across their naked torsos. They were crazy with fear and drugs. You could see the drug patches on their faces. Cocaine. God knows what.

In front of the big house, Chief Keli and some of his elders were squatting on the ground, heads bowed in abjection. Musa Evangeli was standing beside them. His immaculately pressed fatigues and polished shoes made him seem as much a stranger to his own men as to us.

Peremptory and paranoid, his voice carried over the crowd, as if pitched at the very landscape itself.

"You people tried to destroy us. You raised your hands for Tejan Kabba. You raised your hands to bring ECOMOG to this country. You raised your hands to have us killed. We who were your saviors. We risked our lives, waging war against corruption and bad government. You met our kindness with ingratitude and contempt. You gave aid and comfort to our enemies . . ."

The people around me were bewildered. And I too was scarcely able to take in the absurd ramblings of this man as he exhorted us to denounce the traitors among us, to denounce our chief and all who had lent support to the Kabbah government and to ECOMOG.

There was no point in listening. No point in trying to raise one's voice. As if it all had been prearranged, three RUF boys disappeared into the chief's house and dragged a jerrican of petrol out onto the porch. As they spilled the gulping liquid along the gallery and down the steps, Musa Evangeli thundered his ultimatum: "Will you give shelter to our enemies or see your houses burn?"

Then, Chief Keli and several of his big men were forced into the house at gunpoint.

Screams of protest were torn from the throat of the crowd. Some people tried to push their way forward.

"Stop!"

Two RUF boys flung burning brands onto the porch. The shouting ceased. An awed murmuring went through the crowd. Within moments, the entire gallery was engulfed in flame and tarry smoke. Enthralled and dumbstruck, people craned their necks to see.

The flames spread quickly, enfurling the carved verandah posts, fingering the thatch.

We could see the barred door shaking as Chief Keli and the others fought to get out. We could hear their cries.

As smoke twisted across the roof, Musa Evangeli barked new orders

But no longer was the crowd held fast by fear. In a sudden surge, those nearest the burning house rushed toward an unguarded lane. Musa Evangeli was still shouting as the RUF boys behind us opened fire again.

I hunched, gasped, and shut my eyes. My legs buckled. I fell to the ground. Splinters of wood and torn leaves rained down. The gunfire was deafening. And a pall of smoke from the burning house now filled the compound with the livid ambience of an eclipse.

The firing ceased. Intoxicated by their power over us, Musa Evangeli's men shouted and mocked.

I covered my head with my hands and forearms. Above and around me, the foliage of the mango trees was being shredded by a hail of bullets.

Then silence again . . .

I climbed to my feet. The crowd was pouring away in panic. I couldn't see Musa Evangeli, but his men, still firing volleys into the trees, were laughing crazily.

I opened my mouth to say something to Keti Magba, who had been standing next to me. But he was gone. Then, as I looked around, peering through the smoke, I saw Denka.

Shouldered and buffeted by the fleeing crowd, he kept extending a clawed hand in front of him and tilting his head back as if he might grasp by hearing what he was unable to see.

I had hardly started toward him when he staggered and fell.

It was pandemonium now. Dust and smoke obscured everything. People were scattering in all directions. The earth was pulverized. I realized the RUF boys were no longer blocking the lanes. They were actually inciting panic, forcing the exodus.

When I reached Denka I had to yell above the cries and screams.

"Here! This way!"

I pulled him to his feet and grasped his shoulder. His face was caked with red dust. His vacant eyes met mine, his mouth agape, his lower lip quivering. I turned him toward the base of the nearest tree and began guiding him to safety.

"You, stop!"

I pretended not to hear and went on walking the blind man toward the tree.

Suddenly, boots were pounding across the compound. I blinked and hunched my shoulders, waiting to be hit from behind. But my elbow was grabbed and I was swung violently around to confront the bellicose face and curling blackberry lip of one of the young punks who had doused the chief's house with petrol.

"You!" he screamed.

I said nothing. I could not. My body was like stone.

Denka held on to me as though I were a rock.

When the RUF boy hit me, the blow seemed to fall from afar, the stock of the weapon descending in dreadful slow motion, so, when it struck me across the ear and cheek and I was thrown to the ground, I was more astonished than hurt.

I tensed, expecting to be kicked or shot.

"N'Sala! Lef'm!"

I could hardly see for the sweat and dirt in my eyes.

Then, like a figure seen through smoked glass, Musa Evangeli was striding toward me with an expression of what I took to be absolute derision. I knew the end had come. I was a journalist. Journalists had been targeted. Friends of mine had been tortured and killed, accused of passing information to ECOMOG or siding with the Kabbah government. I knew this was the moment of my death. I looked Musa in the eye, waiting for a glimmer of recognition before he ordered N'Sala to kill me. But then he turned, distracted by something he had heard or that had suddenly crossed his mind. And he was striding away with N'Sala loping in his wake like a pariah dog.

Later I would realize that they had gone to supervise the stripping of roofing iron from the houses before they were set on fire.

I limped back to Bala's house, where many of the women who had been shot were lying on the porch, nursed by the women who had remained with them or returned there after the burning of the chief's house. The trampled laterite in the yard was black with blood. A shabby vulture hobbled across the yard like a broken umbrella, fixing us with its beady eyes. Others were sitting on nearby roofs, arching their scrawny necks.

Over Sangbamba the smoke poured skyward. Tongues of flame were spitting sparks high into the air. There was every chance the fire would spread unchecked through the whole western quarter of the village. My childhood house, old Morowa's house, the mosque, would go up in flames. Even if the villagers who had fled came back, there was little they could do. The thatched houses were built too close together. There was no water. And clearly it was Musa Evangeli's intention to raze the village to the ground, leaving us with nothing.

I fell against the wall of the porch. I was trembling with shock. Like a leaf. My mind kept jumping. Strangely, I did not care what became of me. My sole concern was that I had no shirt to wear, not that I might die.

Then, as if he had materialized out of nowhere, Musa Evangeli was standing at the other end of the porch, swigging Coca-Cola. Several of his boys were opening bottles of beer. One began tossing stones at the vultures in the yard. It's bizarre the things you remember. The RUF louts looking like kids who've completed a hard day's work and earned their rest. The filaments of ash drifting out of the sky. The smell of beer. The lurid light. The sobbing and moaning of the wounded women, which clearly troubled some of the RUF boys. One turned to Musa Evangeli and asked what they should do.

He did not reply, but sipped his coke and gazed out over the heads of his boys to where the fires were burning. Once some filigrees of ash fell on his battle fatigues and he flicked them away. He seemed blind to the torn, bloodstained clothing at his feet.

Then an unearthly wailing filled the house.

It visibly affected us all. For a moment we were only human.

A couple of the RUF boys grabbed their weapons. Again they looked to their leader.

This time the mask of indifference fell away.

"Shit!" he said, and hurled his coke bottle into the compound.

At that moment, Sinkari appeared in the doorway. Her eyes were wild. She searched the yard, the porch, then, seeing him, her anger broke.

"Murderer!" she cried. "Murderer!"

For a minute, then, the terrible lamentations in the house seemed to crush her. She collapsed against the doorjamb beside me, wincing with pain.

"No one has ever killed another human being in this village," she cried. "We do not kill human beings here!"

And then, as if her rage was fed by the keening, she tore her lapa from her breast and shouted: 'May you who suckled at your mother's breast never slake your thirst again. May you whose mother gave you food never know the taste of food again. May the sustenance you drew from others be withdrawn from you. May you die without kinsmen or children, like an animal, alone!"

Musa Evangeli ignored her. But his eyes could not meet Sinkari's stare.

Sinkari thrust herself from the doorway and tottered toward the man she had cursed. Her voice was overflowing with the grief and anger of a lifetime.

"You have killed Tina Marafa," she cried. "You! You have murdered her! Others will also die, and you will have murdered them!"

"So we have. Just as you would have killed us, if you had the means."

And then I spoke, desperate to relieve Sinkari of the danger of confronting this man. "Some of these women are not dead," I said. "They are seriously hurt. Are you going to let them die?"

"I don't need advice from you, Mansaray! Who do you think you are? Some kind of hero here? With your bandages and morality. You're nothing to me. You count for nothing now! You're lucky to be alive."

That he recognized me gave me a strange sense of immunity. His invective could not touch me. And I had seen him give. The black shoes scuffed and grubby now. The fatigues sweat-stained and slashed with charcoal. The moment of killing past.

"If we can get those women to Alikalia," I said, "they can be treated. The Red Cross isn't interested in your politics —"

He scowled and looked away toward the western sky where the sun glowed red through the pall of smoke. Behind us the women's keening rose and fell. It seemed to wreak a palpable change on him. Suddenly, he smashed his fist against the porch post. Then, shouting orders, he dispatched two of his men to the other end of the village, saying it was time to leave.

"It'll be dark soon," I said.

"Don't talk to me, Mansaray! Don't you dare talk to me!"

I slumped back against the wall. But I knew I had to speak again. If I let myself be silenced now, I would lose whatever advantage I had gained. But my throat was parched and raw, the side of my head swollen and throbbing with pain.

It was at that moment, out of the blur and fug around me, that my daughter appeared. My first impulse was to order her away. To urge her to hide herself. Not to associate herself with me. But she pressed a mug of water into my hand. I took a sip. Splashed water over my face. The contusion like an air bubble under the skin. It was painful to move my jaw. "You must go now!" I said.

"What did you say to her?" Musa Evangeli barked.

"I asked if she was all right."

"Who is she?"

"She is no one."

"And who are you, Mansaray?"

"I too am no one."

"Yes, you are no one. If you were someone I would have killed you. I would derive satisfaction from killing you. But you are a pitiful nothing. A piece of shit. Worrying about women. Crawling in the dirt! I remember you from school. Groveling to Father Joseph. Always groveling. Dirt was your element then and dirt is your element now. Look at you! Always in the dirt. When you die, they will not have to dig a grave for you. You have already gone back to the dirt from which you were made!"

I had felt strong. I had even imagined I might manipulate him. Now I was the victim of his scorn.

In the false twilight we filed out of Sangbamba. A levy of village women had been pressed into carrying bundles of roofing iron and boxes of looted goods on their heads. And several boys and girls from the village had been roped together, destined for the RUF combat camps. They were behind us. My daughter Mariama was among them. Keti Magba said he had seen her, and I had no reason to doubt him. It was also from him that I learned of what had happened in the Western compounds, the amputations, the killings there. "They told us we had voted for the government that was trying to kill them," Keti Magba said. "Now they would cut off the hands that had voted against them. If we thought this was unjust, we should go to the president and ask for new hands."

Apart from an occasional cry of pain or complaint when someone stumbled, our procession moved in funereal silence. Even Musa Evangeli's men seemed defeated by the events of the day. Musa Evangeli himself I observed only once or twice, walking at the head of the column, towering above the line of red berets that bobbed behind him in the descending darkness.

Climbing the hill where Sangbamba became visible for the last time, I did not look back. I did not want to see the pall of smoke in the night sky. I did not want to think of the fires still burning, my possessions in the smoldering ruins.

So we moved on into the falling night, across the black morass of Bandafon, beneath the great domed inselberg of Inkafode, through a landscape haunted by memories and djinn.

We passed through Timbiran, which the rebels had destroyed on their way to Sangbamba. Other abandoned hamlets came and went in the darkness, and I imagined I could hear the tortured and useless cries of their inhabitants, now absorbed into the uncomprehending landscape. How impotent and pitiful we human beings are in the face of death! How quickly reduced to nothingness. Why, when I could have easily slipped away into the darkness, did I stay with that column? Was it because of some atavistic sense of solidarity, of safety in numbers? Or a fear of doing something that might make matters worse? Or simply the shock of experiences that beggared belief, that went beyond anything I had known before? These questions I still ask myself. But one thing I know. Reason deserts a person at such times.

At Daru we rested. We sat clumped together, oppressed by the dank river air and the stammering roar of the nearby river. I could not have walked another mile. I lay down, clutching myself to keep warm. I wanted to sleep. I wanted it all to be over. But there were shouts and curses from the RUF boys, and the beams of electric torches were jerking about over the trampled grass. Somewhere my daughter was cowering, afraid. I could not bear to think of what lay in store for her. Whether she had been abused already. Of what the morning would bring. Of my own powerlessness to save her.

After a few hours sleep we pressed on. I still had not seen Mariama or the other youngsters. Keti Magba thought that had been detained in Timbiran. Abdul Keita said they been taken elsewhere, earlier. I tried to persuade one of the RUF boys to tell me what had happened. He said he would cut out my tongue if I asked such a question again. So we were fewer now, heading God knows where, goaded along the path and occasionally forced to stand together, while the RUF boys drank or ate, or simply talked together."

"What will they do to us?" Abdul asked me.

I could not answer him. I wanted to keep my thoughts to myself. Besides, we were entering the heart of the forest now, painfully picking our way over fallen logs and outcrops of rock.

We reached Bandamusaia the next night. Beyond lay the foothills and the RUF combat camp. All of us dreaded what would befall us there. But again I refused to discuss the matter. It could only weaken us. It would increase the likelihood of our worst fears becoming reality.

Bandamusaia had been abandoned months before. We were taken to a ruined house. The roofing iron had been stripped from it. Vines had already covered the rafters, and saplings were growing through the broken concrete floors. We were ordered to sit down. One of the RUF boys, whom the others called Blood, showed us how we were to sit, with our legs stretched out in front of us.

I was the first to be bound. Rope was wrapped tightly above my kneecaps, and my wrists tied with the same length of rope. Then masking tape was drawn over my mouth and pulled around the back of my head.

There were about twenty of us. One by one, we were trussed in the same way, then picked up under the armpits and ankles, and slung onto a heap.

I could barely move. I was bone weary. The rope cut into my legs. My head felt as though it had been split open. I was as desperate for a piss as I was for a drink of water. My tongue was swollen. The tape over my mouth was torture. Yet, like the others, I managed to extricate myself from the heap and sit upright. I was determined to die with my face to the night sky and the stars.

We were convinced the end was nigh. But it was the ignominy of it all that appalled me. There was no panic. Only futile outrage, a sense of anticlimax, and the overwhelming realization that our lives were invisible to the boys who would kill us. That we were absolutely nothing to them.

After binding and silencing us, the RUF boys prepared their drugs. We watched as they used razor blades to cut small incisions in one another's cheeks and temples, then rub a whitish power into the cuts. They covered the incisions with masking tape. Some drank omoli. It was not long before we became their foils.

"Heh bo, you smoke?"

The young thug called Abila'u, which means "dangerous thing" in Mandingo, came toward me, clutching a small jerrican.

"You thirsty?"

Hooting with mirth, Abila'u doused us with petrol.

"You want a light?" Abila'u asked me. "Maybe your friend wants a light." Staring straight into my face, he bent forward and stubbed his cigarette out on Abdul's scalp.

Abdul drew in his breath sharply, and I felt his body flinch and stiffen. The acrid smell of singed hair amused Abila'u. Whining in mimicry of a fire siren, he sprinkled more petrol over us. The other thugs howled with laughter.

I was sickened by my own victimhood. I stared at Abila'u. My nostrils flared. A wild guttural noise came from my throat.

"You got something to say?"

Abila'u found the end of the masking tape and ripped it from my mouth. Tears of pain and rage blinded me. I cursed him without thinking.

Abila'u's eyes had difficulty focusing. He kicked me hard.

Trapped between Abdul and Keti Magba, I could not move. I tried to bury my head between my knees, but the rope would not allow it. Abila'u kicked me again and again. I felt nothing. His boots sank into my body as though I were already dead.

---

I stopped reading. For a moment I felt that I had been hearing the voice of the dead and that Ezekiel was a specter. His story came from a region so remote from anything I knew, anything I could conceive, that words were travesties and the terrible arbitrariness of what had happened filled me with shame. When, finally, I did read on, my eyes were blurred with tears.

The account was spare now, recounting the details of how Ezekiel made his escape.

Inexplicably, the rebels left them alone most of that night in Bandamusaia, preferring the entertainment of reggae tapes on a boom box and, finally, sleep. During those hours of reprieve, Ezekiel was able to free himself from his bonds. But, with the exception of Abdul, the others slept or turned their faces away. They preferred to take their chance, they said. They had survived so far. Surely if the RUF wanted them dead, they would have killed them already. Why waste their precious petrol, if they did not intend to burn them alive?

Toward dawn, Ezekiel and Abdul clambered up into the rafters of the house. Fires were still glowing where the RUF boys were camped. The two men slid down the back wall of the house, and slipped noiselessly into the forest. It was unbearably easy. But Ezekiel was badly bruised. It was difficult for him to walk. And he and Abdul wandered for two days, by turns cursing their companions for their cowardice and berating themselves for having left them to their fate. Above all, Ezekiel mourned his daughter. "I prayed for death," he said. "Like my brother, I had run away. Like a child in fright. Thinking only of myself. As soon as I had gone, I realized I was not free at all. But I could not go back. I had lost my only opportunity for death."

I could not sleep that night for thinking of what Ezekiel had suffered, and still suffered. And I could not put out of my mind the thought that his fascination with the RUF was born of his own survivor guilt. It was not a matter of whether the RUF boys could be accepted back into their home communities, but of whether *he* could go home again. It was not a question of whether they could live with the evil they had done, but whether he could. When I asked Ezekiel if he would ever publish his story, the story he had shared with me, he said: "How could I? What happened made everything unreal. My family life, my writing, even this village. Nothing was the same as it was. After such madness, how can one write stories? Sometimes I feel I no longer belong to this world. Is it me here, talking to you, or a ghost? A memory of the person I once was, the life I once had? Life is fire, words are ash."

## Petra's Letter

I found myself contemplating this image many times in the days that followed, as the neophytes returned from the bush to begin their new lives. When Sanfan Fina reappeared at Bala's house, I did not at first recognize her. The bashful, pubescent girl had metamorphosed into a self-possessed young woman. Her braided hair was festooned with red berries. She wore a white country-cloth gown that Bala had sewn for her. And she sat with composure on the steps of the house, smiling at us, as if in triumph. Was this not, I wondered, the example I had been seeking of the baptism of fire, the phoenix risen from the ashes? But, though I drew some comfort from this conceit, I knew it would have been an insult to confide it to Ezekiel. And I remembered those long months at Cambridge when he went walking alone on the fens, undoubtedly turning over and over in his mind the tragic events he had finally decided to share with me.

The following morning, I was squatting beside a hearth in the backyard, poking bits of wood between the firestones in an effort to bring my water quickly to the boil so that I could leave the yard to Sinkari and Mantene again. My eyes were smarting from the smoke, my hands grimy with ash. What, I wondered, did Bala's wives think of my clumsy attempts to perform the simplest task? Mantene was sitting on the ground in the shade of a mango tree. Legs extended straight out in front of her, she was bouncing her baby up and down in her lap while singing softly. Sinkari was sweeping rice husks, peanut shells, and other debris from the tamped earth of the yard with a switch broom. Watching her hobble about made me painfully aware of the misery that had been visited upon this village, yet it was difficult to reconcile the joy on Mantene's face as she played with her baby, or Sinkari's suppleness as she bent to her sweeping, with the harrowing scenes that Ezekiel had described in his manuscript.

"You should let Mantene do that."

I was so startled by Ezekiel's voice, as he emerged from the shadows of the backdoor, that I almost knocked over the pot of now-simmering water that was balanced precariously on the three charred clay hearthstones—symbols, Mantene had informed me earlier, of mother, father, and child.

"Mantene has better things to do with her time than boil my drinking water," I said.

"You embarrass them, you know, invading their space."

"I'm almost done."

Mantene, who had momentarily stopped singing, now resumed. I listened, rapt, for a few moments, before asking Ezekiel to translate the words of her song.

"She is exhorting women to be grateful for their children," Ezekiel said. "Not to anguish over the hardships of conceiving, bearing, and raising them, for a male child will give her a compound and a female child will give her a house."

"Which is more important, compound or house?"

When Ezekiel translated my question, Mantene laughed. "The compound, of course. The compound contains the house."

"So women are contained within the world of men?" I asked.

"Perhaps we should ask Sinkari that?" Ezekiel said wryly.

Sinkari, who had been sweeping steadily and ignoring us, now straightened up and looked sternly at Ezekiel.

"Men could say that," she said.

"And what do women say?"

"What is the word for kinship in our language?" Sinkari demanded to know. "*Nakelinyorgoye*, isn't it? And what is the word for family? *Dembaiye*. Tell that to your stranger."

"*Na* means mother," Ezekiel explained. "Kinsmen are 'mother-ones.' And demba is a nursing mother."

"We could also say that we contain the men," Sinkari said. "We carry them in our bellies, we give birth to them, we feed and nurture them. Where would they be without us?"

Ezekiel then said something to Sinkari that drew an angry and reproachful reaction.

"What did she say?" I asked.

"She asked me if it was a woman who destroyed her foot, so that she cannot walk properly or carry firewood and water on her head without falling. She asked me if it was a woman who burned this village to the ground. And whether it was a woman that murdered her friend Tina Marafa and cut off her younger co-wife's hand."

It was not difficult to imagine her confronting Ezekiel's nemesis, cursing him to his face.

"Luckily for us," Sinkari went on, "God decided to wake up before it was too late, and the war was only one day in the life of this place. Even as those RUF boys ran about burning and killing, we went on with our lives. Life was too much for them. They killed fifteen people here, but they could not put an end to life. Mantene gave birth to her baby son. We made our farms. We fed our children. We kept each other going. And even though we were scattered by the war like chaff from a winnowing tray, we came together again. Did you not see the *biriye?* How we moved together. How we moved as one. How we brought life back into this world. You see this broom? You see me sweeping this yard. Tell him, Ezekiel. Tell him the meaning of the *sundukunye ma.*"

"All the rubbish gets thrown in the backyard," Ezekiel explained. "Sweepings from the house, ash from the cooking fires, rice husks from winnowing, scraps of paper . . . Even the bodies of dead infants are sometimes buried here, under the hearthstones or in the rubbish heap—"

"Have you told him that?" Sinkari interrupted.

"Hmhn."

"Now tell him about the fire finches."

"You have seen those small red birds?" Ezekiel said. "The ones that nest in the eaves of the houses and are always flying about in the backyard? We say that the souls of children who die before they are weaned go into the birds and may be reincarnated. That is why we bury the dead babies in the rubbish heap or under the firestones. The point is, you see . . . the point she is making is that new life is sometimes born from the rubbish heap. From where you least expect it."

"So life goes on.

"So life goes on."

"And what of those who did these terrible things? Does their life also go on?"

"That is not for us to say. That is up to God."

As in confirmation of Ezekiel's fatalism, news reached the village that same day of the death of Musa Evangeli's father in Alkalia.

We were sharing a place of rice with a sauce of mashed cassava leaf, chili, and dried fish.

"Will Musa attend the funeral?" I asked.

"Musa is also dead," Ezekiel said. And he recalled how, at school, Bala and he had addressed him as "elder brother." "He was always very quiet. He kept his thoughts and feelings to himself. I don't know why he changed. But change he did. It broke his father's heart. Even before Musa fled to Liberia and got caught up in the fighting there and was killed. Yet they never got on, father and son. When Musa was a boy, the father was always badgering him, telling him he was useless, putting him down. Perhaps it was a ruse, to disguise from his other sons the fact that Musa would inherit everything when the old man died. Perhaps it was ill will. But Musa took it very hard. That I do know. He complained bitterly at the way his father lectured him constantly on the virtues of hard work and perseverance. Praise had to be earned, gifts deserved. Nothing came from nothing. I lost track of him about the time I went to Freetown. We moved in very different circles. But I heard he attended Fourah Bay College for a while, and was politically active in protests against the ANC government. Then there were rumors that he had gone to Libya to train as a guerrilla. Certainly the man who confronted me in Sangbamba was not the Musa I knew. And it was clear he was not fighting for a cause any longer; he was fighting to save his own skin. Even now I do not bear him a grudge. He had a vision of what this country could be. But in trying to realize his vision he destroyed the lives of thousands of innocent people. His life was a life of our times."

"How can you be so forgiving," I asked. "Given what happened here?"

"We have a saying, Tom. Speech burns the mouth; in silence hearts grow cool again. What good would it do us to nurse our wounds, to recount these stories of what we suffered, to punish and ostracize those who took the wrong path? You saw Sanfan Fina when she came back from the bush? You saw the happiness in her face. You saw the mothers of the other girls, dancing here night after night. Their faces aglow with pride. As Sinkari said, 'This is how life goes on.'"

"But what of the boys? What of Yandi, for example?"

"It is harder for them, to be sure. The girls have their destinies as mothers. They are raised to that. But for the young boys, many have nothing to look forward to, no one to look up to. When they look around and see the Big Men in power—all that corruption and greed—they feel betrayed. Then they see their fathers, making their farms, doing the same as their fathers did before them, and they want more than that for themselves and for their sons. Whose footsteps will they follow? Yandi looks to me. Others have no guides, no allies. They drift away from the villages, they go into the army or in search of diamonds or to the cities, looking for a door through which they can pass into a better life. But it is easier for a camel to pass through the eye of a needle than for them to find their way in this world. No wonder they grow bitter. Why should their dreams come to nothing? Why should their lives be endless waiting? Why should they be shut out when others have everything! It is not difficult to understand the boys who joined the RUF. They wanted to be men. But their desire for manhood was sidetracked. It became fixated on a misguided tyrant. They called Foday Sankoh "Pappy." You see what I mean? What children they were, even in their desperation to become men!

The following morning, Ezekiel announced calmly that he was going back to Freetown for a while. Did I want to accompany him?

Nothing was further from my mind, and I asked if it would be all right if I stayed on, as Bala's "stranger."

Ezekiel seemed relieved. Perhaps he needed a break, not only from Sangbamba but from my dependency upon him. Promising to return soon, he asked if there was perhaps something he could bring back for me.

I asked only that he post a letter I had written to Petra and try to get some medicines for me to dispense: chloromycetin, electrolyte solution, aspirin, antibiotics. I also needed a pair of sturdier shoes and, if possible, some real coffee.

Two days later, a cousin of Ezekiel's turned up in Sangbamba with my mail.

I took the brown paper package from him with trepidation, dreading the anxious demands it would undoubtedly contain from friends and family and my supervisor.

The first letter took me by surprise. It was from Cosmega. A handwritten note on a page of Croxley Bond in which she expressed concern for my well-being and assured me of a warm welcome when I came back to Freetown. After sorting through the remaining letters in my room, I tossed the ones from Johns onto my bedside table, then headed out of the village to my refuge among the rocks and long grass on the hill. There, in the shade of a twisted lophira tree, and with a trembling hand, I peeled back the flap of the envelope containing Petra's letter.

Dear Tom,

For several days after your departure I was in a state of deep shock. I had no way of knowing if our relationship was over or simply on ice or even if you were in the land of the living. When you first told me of your plans to go to Africa, I felt rejected and angry, though I tried not to show my feelings, wanting to give you support in what was obviously a difficult time for you. After you left, I did not know what to think. All manner of scenarios presented themselves to my mind, besieging and obsessing me. I was desperate for news from you. Every time the phone rang I thought it surely must be you. Any scrap of news would have been better than nothing. I didn't know where I stood, what kind of future I faced, or what on earth you were doing. Then came your card. That minimalist communication was, in some ways, worse than nothing. But at least I had an address and could write, even though I have no way of knowing whether you will receive this letter or even bother to reply . . .

I began this letter last week. I wrote the above, then stopped. I did not know what else to say. But over the last few days I have suddenly and inexplicably felt free. Even though we are in the depths of winter here, I wake to the day with impatience and joy. I am filled with strength. I feel strangely immune. I speak my mind. I feel like a goddess, invincible, the kind of thing Conrad talks about—"the feeling that I could last forever, outlast the sea, the earth, and all men." The feeling that I am what I am—myself in my own right. That everything touches me because nothing touches me. The complete negation of the ego, the complete submergence in everything that is not me, the loss of pride and selfness—the feeling that I have outstripped myself to become myself. Is all this true? I am very conscious that all this is written to you, Tom, and not for my own gratification. It does not gratify me at all to write it. It is an effort that is tearing me apart. I don't know even how you will feel about it. It might be your means of repudiating me completely, for all I know. I have had to dissociate myself from the part of me that is you to write it. That is why I have no notion as to how you will react. I write as honestly as I can, without embellishment, hoping you will see in it the core that is me and accept or reject that core and not the clothing upon it which you may think of as me. Anyway, I suppose something in me has decided that I will live as though you did not exist, perhaps as you have decided to live without me. I have renewed old friendships. Others have deepened. My affections, unfocused on you or me, have become diffuse. I feel great love for everyone. Sylvia has been a tower of strength. I always thought of her as weak and needy; but she has proven herself to be quite otherwise. I have thrown myself into work. And in the weekends I go down to London and stay with Faith and Bob, or simply enjoy the town, shopping, going to the theater, sometimes seeing a movie.

Now I have really run out things to say!

I will end with some lines from Widsmith that I was rereading the other day. For some reason they brought you to mind.

*The makar's weird is to be a wanderer:*
*The poets of mankind go through the many countries,*
*Speak their needs, say their thanks.*
*Always they meet with someone, in the south lands or the north,*
*Who understands their art, an open-handed man*
*Who would not have his fame fail among the guard*

*Nor rest from an earl's deeds before the end cuts off light and life*
*together . . .*
Write if you will. And know I love you.
Petra
PS. I enclose some other personal letters and a couple of things from
Johns that seemed urgent; I haven't opened any of them. And I hope I'm
not taking a huge risk by sending them. Someone told me there are no
proper postal or telephone services in Sierra Leone because of the war. I
can't imagine such a place. Please take care.

It was impossible to bridge the gap between myself and this other life.
As I made my way slowly down the hill, the dry grass brushing against my
jeans, I felt that I existed nowhere now. These voices were from another life.
Afterimages at best. And, as with hallucinations, I believed that my sanity
depended on my giving them no credence.

Was it this disenchantment with words, this sense that I was dying to everything I had known before, that persuaded me to accompany Ezekiel's nephew
to the Loma mountains . . . movement, any kind of movement, preferable
to sitting still? Did this journey offer an escape from the boredom that now
afflicted me as I sat for hours on Bala's porch, observing the routines of the
village like the old men who sat outside the pub at Todmorden when I was a
boy, watching the world go by? Occasionally Bala and I attempted a conversation, in a mix of Krio and English, only to abort it as we came up against the
limits of our language. Sometimes I strolled about the village, greeting people
or whiling away the time in convivial silence with Morowa, the old medicine
master. Mostly, however, I sat for hours on end as if in a trance.

Yet I was not alone in succumbing to the lassitude of the season. Harvest
was done. The men lounged in their hammocks or held desultory conversations with neighbors that I could barely follow. A young man, who Yandi
said had been abducted by the RUF during the war, patiently wove bamboo
mats in Bala's compound, threading the carefully split cane through a grid
of raffia strings that were tied to small stakes in the ground. One day, in
the course of an aimless conversation, he said: "Many years ago, the white
man came to Saralon and took us away to his country against our will; now

when we want to go, he will not let us." A second man, who spoke little, set up his weaving frame in the shade of the orange tree where Sanfan Fina had braided her hair before her initiation, and as others slept during the heat of the day he added to his long narrow strip of white country cloth and wound it into a tight ball. Images, I thought, of Penelope's web. Of the web of perpetual waiting.

If I took an evening stroll outside the village, I would meet the women as they came and went along the path that led to their section of the local stream. Momentarily captivated by the grace with which they carried pails of water on their heads, the coy smiles they threw me or their sudden gusts of laughter, I would also be shamefully aware of their mocking comments, for once again the *tubabune* had invaded their space. If I retired to my room, I would lie on my bed and stare at the ceiling, listening to the ping ping of the roofing iron as it expanded in the heat or contracted as night fell. I wrote less and less in my journal. Ezekiel's story had exhausted me. So when Yandi told me that he had to go on an errand to Bandamusaia, I immediately expressed an interest in accompanying him.

A lanky, sinewy boy of about fifteen, Yandi had always kept his distance from me. Ezekiel's explanation was that his nephew was afraid I would find his English wanting. So I was not surprised when Yandi responded to my suggestion with an embarrassed silence.

"I would like to see the mountains," I explained.

The apprehensive look on Yandi's face only deepened.

"I will ask my uncle," Yandi said.

"But he is in Freetown," I said.

"My uncle Bala."

"Let me ask him," I said.

Bala's reaction was even more negative than his nephew's. He frowned. He pretended he could not understand my request. He said it was dangerous for a white man in the mountains. He escaped into silence. But I was determined to brook no argument. And so, despite Yandi's reluctance and Bala's annoyance, I got my way.

We set off before daybreak on a journey that would retrace Ezekiel's steps in 1998 after the sacking of Sangbamba.

In the grasslands, the moonlight showed us the path. Yandi walked ahead, his bare feet padding on the dusty ground. Twice, nightjars flew up from the path where they had been resting, startling us. It prompted me to ask Yandi if he had been in Sangbamba when the rebels came.

"No, I was in Alikalia with my cousins at that time."

"Were you in school?"

"Yes."

Mindful of what Ezekiel had told me about his own schooldays at the mission, I asked Yandi what he hoped to do with his education, to which he answered, "I want to help people; I want to be like my uncle Ezekiel."

"What kind of job would you like to have?"

"I want to be a teacher, like my uncle."

"I also hope to be a teacher one day."

"Yes, my uncle told me."

"But I will not teach people to read and write. Not like Ezekiel."

"What will you teach?"

"Nothing very useful I'm afraid."

"You can come and teach in Sangbamba."

"But there is no school."

"There was a school. But the RUF burned it down."

As the sun rose, we shared the peppery venison and cassava that Mantene had prepared against our journey. Then we pressed on toward the mist-swathed forests along the Yimalan.

It was like entering a cage, filled with cackling and hooting animals. Had our journey been dreamt, it would have been interpreted as a sign that a plot had been hatched against us. Neither of us spoke. Perhaps it was because we had been walking for so long in the hypnotic circlets of lantern light. Perhaps it was because we unconsciously deferred to the spirits of the forest who, according to Yandi, could capture our names and use them to do us harm.

The path led through swamps. The mist clung to us. The stench of decaying vegetation was overpowering. In the distance the rapids of the Yimalan ransacked the trees like a high wind.

It was noon when we entered Timbiran. Yandi introduced me to the town chief and explained to him where we were going, though not why. Then we plunged once more into the forest, stumbling over exposed roots and outcrops of stones, getting closer to the river.

The Yimalan marked the western boundaries of the chiefdom. Overhanging trees and lianas threw shadows across the turbid water. Yandi said that crocodiles lurked in the deep pools, but all I saw animate the sullen surfaces was the dappling sunlight and falling leaves. He also pointed out the trail that diamond smugglers used. "They make a dog swallow the stones," Yandi said, "or they put them in a banana and eat it themselves. Sometimes the women put them in those cloths, the ones they use when they are bleeding . . ."

We crossed the river on a hammock bridge and entered forest even more dense and overpowering than before. The narrow path was aswarm with ants. Myriads of butterflies illuminated the occasional shafts of sunlight. Green tree snakes slowly uncoiled along the trail, and the spoor of monkeys could be seen everywhere.

"Are diamonds still smuggled through here?" I asked.

"I should not say."

"Why shouldn't you?"

"I am not permitted to say."

"Who won't permit you to say?"

"My uncle Bala."

It was then that I began to wonder about the object of Yandi's errand and to ask myself why Bala's house had been left intact on the day of the RUF raid and why Bala had been able to slip away so easily and what other intrigues lay beneath the seemingly placid surface of life in Sangbamba. Though such suspicions were undoubtedly symptoms of the mild paranoia that sometimes took hold of me, unable to catch the drift of everyday conversations, divine people's unspoken expectations, or read between the lines, it was probably inevitable, being a stranger to that place, that I would fall foul of my own worst imaginings.

We reached Bandamusaia in the heat of the day.

The chief explained that he was accustomed to having white men lodge in his village. They used to make it their base, before scaling the Loma Mountains. But I was the first white man to have passed that way in many years, which undoubtedly explained why the small children of the village, some stark naked, some in rags, fled in fear from my presence, only to be dragged back by their older siblings and shoved before me, their eyes wide with alarm.

The village was clustered beneath an immense granite escarpment. Blackened and eroded by rain, this intimidating wall of rock was like a materialization of the darkness. Yandi hastened away in search of his kith and kin, and to deliver his messages, while I attempted to make myself at home in the derelict house that had been provided for my accommodation—the same house, perhaps, from which Ezekiel made his escape from the RUF.

I lit a fire in the yard and boiled some water in the small country pot I found there. Then I sat on the front porch—or what remained of it—with a cup of tea clutched between my hands, hoping that Yandi would soon return with something to eat. Not far away, two mangy goats were nibbling at the grass. I picked up a stone and lobbed it toward them. One had a deformed hind hoof, and it limped away to safety, bleating pitifully. The other joined it, hovering and trembling, in the shadows of another ruined house.

It was dusk by the time Yandi reappeared, carrying a calabash of parboiled rice and a peanut and chili sauce on his head. Having discharged his obligation, he left.

"I will see you in the morning," I said hopefully.

I could not sleep. I had scraped a hollow in the hard earth for my hip, and pummeled my rucksack into the shape of a pillow, but I could not rest. At first I was unnerved by the silence. Then, from the far end of the village, came the sound of wooden clappers, followed by a dull, hoarse muttering, as though someone were stuffing words into the mouth of a horn. My fretfulness gave way to real fear as the sound came closer, but then silence fell again, and I heard only the unsteady thumping of my heart and the intermittent shrieking of a night bird in the bush.

As the night dragged on I succumbed to panic—over what I would write to my adviser, whose letter had demanded that I send immediate details of my work-in-progress and my plans, over whether I should let Petra go, and with her my Cambridge life. When at last I dozed off it was only to wake in a cold sweat from a dream of a clear blue sky suddenly darkened by smoke or cloud. Ezekiel was standing in a line of men and women, waiting his turn to have his hand severed by the RUF. No one spoke. There was no sound. But Ezekiel was begging for his hand. "Don't cut it off," he implored. "With this hand I will write your story. I will take your grievances to the world. I will make your name. You will get money. People in England and America will talk about you. With this hand I can give you a new life. But without my hand I can do nothing. You may as well kill me." And then I realized that Ezekiel was like Scheherazade in *The Arabian Nights*, except that instead of telling stories to the person who had the power of life and death over him, Ezekiel would record that man's story, and the story of others, buying another day of life with every tale he set down . . .

As dawn broke, I got up and paced about, shivering with cold and tearing at my skin. I was now convinced I had spent the night in the same house from which Ezekiel had escaped from the RUF and that his spirit had entered my dreams.

I passed the day in a stupor, but still could not sleep. I was now besieged by fragments of long-forgotten poems, passages from novels I had read as an undergraduate, and hallucinatory flashbacks to Cambridge. Haunting and ephemeral, like episodes from a dimly remembered movie.

As darkness fell and my second night in Bandamusaia began, I struggled to get comfortable and prayed for sleep. Yandi appeared in the half-light for a moment, took one look at me, and left. Perhaps he was afraid of me. Even I was afraid—of going mad or dying. I lay in a delirium, a sodden log drifting on the stream, the air warm and cloying, experiencing slight vertigo as the current rolled me this way and that. I thought: I am not lying on the earth; the earth is suffering my lying upon it. I am disembodied now watching myself lying on the ground, but I am not lying there. I have been placed here, to suffer the darkness, claustrophobic, hot, and the shrilling of a single cicada, but I am not feeling anything or hearing anything. These things are happening to me. I am having them happen to me. Then I was looking down at my own supine body, my awareness drifting away from it like smoke upward through the shattered roof, toward the stars, and I found myself looking back with a kind of calm pity on my abandoned body, thinking: *I am dying, is this dying?* Because I knew I could choose, that I could go back into that prone form if only I made the effort.

In the pitch darkness I wandered around the village calling Yandi's name. When he finally appeared, I told him that I was setting off to Sangbamba immediately and, if necessary, alone. He protested. He wanted to go back to sleep. But in the end he said he would go with me. It was what his uncle would have wanted him to do.

In the lantern's dull penumbra, dark forms stir into life. I am aware of myself walking, of Yandi's presence in the half-light ahead, but I am not so much moving as being moved, as in a dream. Out of the depths of the forest, howls and shouts give voice to scampering shadows.

Not a word passes between us. I walk in a daze. I think only of what I will do when we get back to Sangbamba.

At Daru we rest for a few hours. I catch some sleep in the town chief's house, stretched out on a raffia prayer mat. The first sound sleep for two nights. I wake to an enamel plate of pineapple slices and bananas. Even Yandi seems to feel relief now, nearing home. This strange white man, with his woes and silences, no longer a burden. And the forest already giving way to patches of open grassland, the mist lifting.

We stop again at the Yimalan, and I clamber down the riverbank, strip, and wade into the unmoving water. It is cold. It momentarily shakes the fever out of me and brings me to my senses. On a boomerang-shaped beach, swallow-tailed butterflies quiver and flap in the early morning sunlight before settling back on the dung. In the shade nearby lies the sloughed-off skin of a snake.

## No Condition Is Permanent

Within a day of getting back to Sangbamba I gathered together my meager belongings, thanked Bala and the town chief for their hospitality, and set off on the long trek to Alikalia. There I was lucky enough to find a lorry going south. For a few thousand leones I could ride in the back among sacks of rice. Though the dust was suffocating, and the grain sacks gave little cushioning as the vehicle jolted over the potholed road, I could at least find consolation in the lorry's logo: *No condition is permanent.*

It was late in the day when I reached Freetown and made my way to International Services in Garrison Street. Nothing had changed. The staff, still slumbering at their desks, heads in their arms, came slowly to consciousness, like drugged lizards, and assured me that the power was on and I could make my call to the UK.

As luck would have it, someone in the office at Newnham knew Petra and brought her to the phone. Ignoring her exclamations of surprise, I told her how sorry I was that I had let so many weeks pass without getting in touch. "There are no phones working here. Nothing at all up-country where I have been. No mail services either. Though I got your letter."

"Of course," she said.

"I can't tell you what a relief it is," I said, "to find you in. I must have walked more than forty miles in the last forty-eight hours and I've been on the back of a truck for the last nine. It's hard to believe I'm finally here, talking to you."

"Where's here?"

"Freetown, I'm back in Freetown. I've only just got in."

The connection was bad. There was some kind of delay in my voice reaching Petra, and in hers coming back to me, so that we kept colliding vocally, our voices overlapping and breaking up. Yet I did not want to stop talking for too long, lest we lose the connection or she replace the receiver thinking I had finished the call.

Her voice was remote and uncertain. "My hands are shaking," she said. "You will have to forgive me. You calling, out of the blue like this, after so long. Why don't you talk while I try to calm down. It's impossible for us both to talk anyway."

So I recounted something of the weeks I had spent in Sangbamba, said how moved I had been to receive her letter, and told her of the visions I had of her during my miserable sojourn in the mountains. "I thought I would die," I said, "and that I would never see you again."

"You are much too theatrical, Tom. You frighten me one minute and idealize me the next. I cannot imagine where you are, what you are doing. And you . . . you almost seem to have forgotten who I am! Didn't you read my letter?"

"I thought you were with someone else."

"You didn't understand at all, did you?"

"Didn't I?"

There was a long silence. I thought we had been cut off.

"Are you . . ." I began.

"Are you going to stay much longer?"

"I want to build a school in Sangbamba."

"A school? How on earth will you find the resources to build a school?

"I will build it the same way that people here build their houses. I am convinced it can be done. I thought you might like to help by sending teaching materials. Books. Anything.

"Tom, I respect what you are doing. But please don't ask me to be a part of it. I have my own life here. It has cost me a great deal to recover from your going away. Don't ask any more of me. I cannot give it right now. You must do what you want to do alone. As I must. Do you understand? It has nothing to do with being with anyone else."

A perverse resolve took possession of me as I walked away from Garrison Street, past crowded stalls, gridlocked poda-podas, and locust trees whose withered pods had been crushed underfoot, their seeds scattered. I was burning with anger, the hurt anger of a child who feels that he or she has been hard done by or deprived of some promised boon. She's right, I told myself, *you must do what you want to do alone.* But the very thought was like a stake driven through my heart.

My self-righteous indignation continued to smolder in my brain and body all the way to Cosmega's house, squashed in the backseat of a battered taxi belching blue smoke from its broken muffler. All through that night, fighting off weariness, I scribbled in my journal, searching for clarity. But it did not come. Instead, I was swept away . . .

The children are at school, the servants dismissed. She finds me in my room. I am no longer in possession of myself. I am stirred and swayed by something I cannot prevent.

We exchange no words. She slips off her sandals and pads barefoot to the window. She draws the curtains. The room is filled with a warm light. I can hear the blood coursing in my veins like the sea.

We begin to undress. I marvel at her suppleness, the fluency with which she bends her arm back to unclasp her dress. She is ebony. I am bleached like driftwood.

Murmuring mindlessly, we embrace. I inhale the strangely acrid odor of her armpits. Our bodies are wet. We slip together, clay on a potter's wheel, shaped by each other's hands. We fall onto the bed, bruising each other with kisses. Her tongue quests in my mouth. Greedily my hands feel for her thighs, knead her buttocks, run up and down her spine. She fumbles for my penis. She draws me to her. With a gasp of pleasure I slip into her. We thresh wildly, fucking without tenderness or restraint. Our lips bleed. Her breasts are smeared with my saliva. Her juices flow and slurp as I thrust into her. She claws my back. I breathe her hair, the smell of singed grass. We roll over and over. We flow like water. She sits astride me, rising up and down while I massage her breasts with the heel of my hand. My splayed fingers dig into her shoulders, her pectorals. I feel no urge to come. We fall onto our sides. She begins to pant and squeal, and seizes my wrist, forcing me to move faster, harder. Then she begins to gasp for breath, and flinging my hand away envelops me in her thighs and crushes me to her. And as she cries out I let myself come, charging her with all the pent energy of months, moaning as my seed drains from me, as my loins pump and jerk with a reflex that goes on and on, until I am limp, surfeited, spent.

I loosen and unfold. She lies outstretched, her arms above her head in a gesture of surrender. The breathless air is permeated with the smell of salt and sperm.

I doze off, thinking of the sea. Of being buoyed on a body of turquoise water, riding the swell. Then come awake with a soft jolt, aware she is watching me. I kiss her eyebrows, trace the broad line of her lips with my fingertips. She presses her breasts against my ribs and imprints my forehead with a kiss.

Again I doze, my body remembering the road I traveled yesterday, the lurching of the truck, the lophira plains.

She is the first to speak.

"I'm glad we did it."

"Why? Because now you and Ezekiel can call it quits?"

"That is not it."

I did not believe her. It did not matter. I wasn't fool enough to let myself think that an adolescent Englishman, all things being equal, would have been Cosmega's first choice.

Outside, in the yard, a rooster crowed. A rusty, rasping noise that died in its throat.

She said: "You're the only white man I have ever slept with. But I don't think of you as white."

"I don't think of you as black."

"My girlfriends and I used to think that white people smelled like stale soap."

"Is that what I smell like?"

She laughed, showing her white teeth. She said: "I remember the first time I touched a white person's hair. It made me shudder, it was so soft and thin."

I could feel Cosmega's hair in the palm of my hand, like a memory.

"What did you think about white skin?"

"I thought white people looked sick. I thought all the color had drained out of them."

"I didn't have a mirror in Sangbamba. For seven weeks I didn't see my own face. When I looked at myself in the mirror this morning I half expected to see an African face."

"When I was a girl, I shook hands with a white person and as I stretched out my arm I got a shock because it was black." Cosmega fell silent. Then she said, "You're thinking of your girlfriend, I can understand. You are in love with her and you feel you are deceiving her."

"Don't you feel you are deceiving Ezekiel?"

"No," she said defensively. "I'm not in love with Ezekiel, and we haven't slept together for three years."

"You must have been in love once."

"I was. But not with Ezekiel. It was someone I knew long before I met him."

"What happened?"

"His name was Juno. He wanted to marry me. Then Ezekiel came along and pestered me until I gave in. He kept telling me Juno was mixed up with diamond smuggling, and it was only a matter of time before he got caught. He was always saying things about Juno. I didn't know what to think. I was very young. And he scared me. His moods scared me. I don't know why I married him. I didn't even like him very much."

I wanted to console her, but felt only pity. I said it was late, I needed to get some sleep. When she walked barefoot from the room, dragging her clothes across the floor, I felt immense relief.

---

"You must understand, he's an African man, Tom. African men want their wives to stay home so they can go out and have a good time. We get used to the arrangement. We African wives always do!" She fidgeted with her necklace and glanced over her shoulder as if to confirm that the children were fast asleep. "But Ezekiel never had any real regard for me. Whatever I wanted led to a battle of wills between us. He hated me working. He hated me visiting my parents. He insisted I stay home with the children. 'Who will cook and take care of the house if I am not there?' Even now, he absolutely refuses to allow me to go up-country. He says it is still too dangerous. He says he is thinking of the children. But he is thinking of himself, of what people will say if his wife strikes out on her own."

We were in the kitchen. Cosmega was preparing a meal of dried fish, cassava leaf, and chili sauce for me as she continued her confessional.

"I am happy you and Ezekiel are friends," she said. "I am sure you helped him when he was in England, when he needed help. I am sure there is trust between you. But I cannot trust him. The trust between us is gone forever."

I was finding it difficult to hear her grievances. In marriage as in all things there are always two sides to any story. But Cosmega was persistent, weaving her spell, drawing me closer and closer to her version of the truth.

"A few years ago I had a call from a friend who nurses at the Jallo Hospital. Something had confused her. Ezekiel had turned up and checked a

Mrs. Mansaray into the maternity unit. My friend knew I wasn't pregnant, so she rang the house to find out what was wrong. She was surprised when I answered the phone. How could I be here and there at the same time? Then she told me about this second Mrs. Mansaray—"

Cosmega looked at me cagily, as if searching out my response.

"—the awful thing was, it wasn't even her first child with Ezekiel. She had already borne him a daughter. He had built them a house somewhere up-country—"

"So what did you do?" I said, feigning interest.

"I confronted him! But do you know what he said? He said that all African men of substance had more than one wife. It was customary."

"But you still see each other. You are not divorced?"

"Why should I get divorced? I do not want to marry again. We marry for children. Not for love."

There was such hardness in her. But no hate. She did not allow herself to lose herself in the things that threatened to undo her. Nothing pooled or festered in her heart. And I thought then of Sinkari and of the women of Sangbamba, defying the rebels with their song. The same women I had watched night after night, dancing in a circle in front of Bala's house, shuffling together, bodies pressed against bodies, infants asleep on their backs, turning their haughty yet impassive faces toward me as if to say, we are the ones who suffer, yet we endure, closing the circle, kindling the fire, forming the line, tending the fields, raising the children, seeing that life goes on. And you envy us. You know that we bring life into the world and you do not. You lust after our bodies. You spurn and decry us in your stories. You like to imagine we are weak. That we will run in panic when a snake enters the compound. Yet your names, your lineages, would die out without us. You want us. You do not want us. And yet you cannot get us out of your minds.

That afternoon, Cosmega suggested we take the children to the beach.

The waves were like blades shearing the blue-green water. As the children were engulfed; they cried out and flailed their arms. Wave after wave tumbled them up the steeply shelving beach.

Cosmega walked to and fro, calling to them to take care. Then she strolled idly and gracefully into the water, broaching the combers with down-pressed palms, rising on tiptoes and half turning to me before she let herself sink slowly into the swell.

I trudged back up the beach. The saline crust of the sand cracked under my feet. I lay in the shade of the cassuarinas. Witch-crabs scuttled and scampered away over the white sand.

When Cosmega came out of the sea, I coveted her without qualms — her voluptuous body, wide hips, the globules of seawater on her black skin like oil. I wanted to lick the salt from her shoulders, the wiry black hair in her armpits, her neck. My penis warmed and hardened as though she had touched me. I closed my eyes, thinking how, when I desired her, I found no fault in her, yet afterward felt such waste, vacuity, and sham that even sleep could not relieve it.

I knew I had to go. But days passed and lassitude overwhelmed me. When I thought of Sangbamba, I balked and made excuses, and waited, as I had always done, for fate to rescue me from myself and show me the way.

The inevitable happened. As soon as Ezekiel got wind of the fact that I was staying at Cosmega's, he left a message for me to phone him on his mobile. Our terse conversation lasted no longer than it took to agree that the Majestic was probably the only place downtown that I could find my way to without difficulty. By the time I set Cosmega's cell phone back on the table, my hands were shaking and I did not see how I could possibly go through with the meeting.

Ezekiel arrived before me and was sitting in a red vinyl chair in the hotel lobby. He did not get up. His face was gaunt and tense. I did not even attempt to shake his hand, but slipped abjectly into a second chair, positioned some distance away.

I said: "Before you say anything, there's something you should know."

"Cosmega has already told me."

"I didn't think you two were on speaking terms."

"You forget, my friend. I am married to this woman. She is the mother of my children."

I was in no position to argue. And instinctively I gave ground, as if this might give him back his stolen dignity.

"I thought we were friends," Ezekiel said.

"I like to think we still are."

He sneered.

I said: "I thought you and Cosmega were estranged. You both gave me to understand that you live apart, that you have—"

"Is a wife no longer a wife when her husband is not with her?"

"I have no intention of going on . . ."

"Do what you will. It makes no difference to me. I only implore you to be discrete. Not to spoil my name. Not to bring disgrace upon my children."

In the shadows at the back of the lobby, beside a broken drink-dispensing machine, two emaciated dogs had begun coupling. As the bitch stood her ground with ridiculous indifference, the male absentmindedly rocked and shuddered against her rump. Ezekiel threw a bottle cap at them. But the male only turned his drugged and pleading eyes toward us a little, while the bitch shifted the position of her front legs.

I felt sick with embarrassment. But Ezekiel laughed.

"Sex is all about revenge," he said.

"I want to go back to Sangbamba," I said.

"I won't be there."

"I still want to go back. I have decided to rebuild the school."

"To salve your conscience."

"To give a little."

The two dogs had flopped onto the torn linoleum. The male was licking its penis.

"What do you mean, give?"

"To do something useful. To make a contribution."

"I know what give means, Tom."

"Then what's your problem?"

"Your problem, my friend, not mine. The problem of your history. The problem of your heritage. Of four hundred years of being what you call a great power, of seeing the rest of the world as your domain. You English are so concerned with saving your own souls, you forget that doing good for others is nothing more than a pretext for doing good for yourselves. Don't you see what you are doing? Don't you see how you are trapped in your own history? Seeking your own salvation at our expense!"

"And you, Ezekiel! Am I to interpret the help you give Yandi and Sanfan Fina as an oblique way of seeking forgiveness for abandoning your daughter to a fate worse than death!"

"To hell with you, Tom!

"What gives you the right to question my motives, then? What makes you any less a victim of circumstance than I?"

"Because I know you, my friend. And because you have shown your true colors. In *my* house. The house where my children live."

"I like to think I know you too, Ezekiel."

"Go back to Sangbamba, then. For all the good it will do you."

Cosmega was sitting alone in the parlor when I returned. She was watching a video. She regularly rented them from a Lebanese shop in Pademba Road. Pirated kung fu movies, Nigerian action movies, soft porn. A curious mix, one would have thought, in the wake of a brutal civil war.

I picked up the cassette box and read *Family Secrets*.

"It's a true romance," Cosmega explained.

"What about this one?" I asked. It was called *Revenge in August*.

"Suspense," Cosmega said.

I asked her how her day had been.

Without switching off the video, she said she'd attended a funeral while I was in town.

"Someone you knew well?"

"She was a friend."

A few days ago, Cosmega's friend admitted herself to the military hospital to deliver her ninth child. She hemorrhaged during the delivery. Her doctor was not in attendance and had left no contact phone number or address. The young woman bled from eleven at night until eight in the morning. There was no blood bank. It hadn't even been possible to check her blood-type.

"Where was her husband?"

"In Kenema. He got back today, just in time to miss her funeral."

I shook my head in disbelief.

"Your food is there," Cosmega said, indicating the pyrex dishes of dried fish and rice on the table. Then her attention went back to the video.

# The School

The day I returned to Sangbamba, Bala told me that his father had appeared to him in a dream. In the dream his father had been rebuilding a house. I told Bala that I too had had a dream. In my dream it was the school that was being rebuilt.

"Then that is it," Bala said.

The course of things was no longer in my hands. I did not have any sense that I had decided to rebuild the school; the task had fallen to me. Nor had I chosen to return to Sangbamba; rather, to Sangbamba I had been returned.

With Yandi's help I began the backbreaking task of making mud bricks. Taking cues from Bala, we first marked out the perimeter of the schoolhouse by hammering small stakes into the ground and joining them up with raffia string. We then calculated how many bricks we would need for walls that would stand about four feet high. I wanted there to be an open space between the top of the walls and the roof, to allow air to circulate and to prevent the kids from feeling walled in.

We used four-sided wooden forms, filling them with clay we dug from the hill and water from the Yimele Stream. Mantene enlisted the help of some of her age-mates, who fetched the water for us, and, as progress was made, other villagers pitched in with advice, with stints digging clay, mixing the mud, filling the form boxes, and upturning the wet bricks on the ground to dry. My hope was that we could produce at least fifty a day.

I could have done nothing without Yandi's assistance. Not only did he labor throughout the day without complaint, he was my translator and constant companion. Though we had little to say to each other beyond the tasks that absorbed us, we became as one, simply by working together toward a common goal.

Against the deafening pulse of cicadas, my axe echoed in the clearing. When Yandi and I had cut enough poles, we stripped the bark from them. Next day, we toted them back to the village. On narrow paths, men waited for me to pass. They greeted us. We greeted them. The work was done.

Over the next few days we cut grass for the roof, and one of Yandi's age-mates set to work making mats for the ceilings.

In the heat of the afternoon, while the village dozed, I went down to the stream to wash. Shedding my filthy clothes, I sank naked into the tepid water. Using a loofa, I scrubbed at the dirt around my ankles and knees. My body ached. But I was utterly at peace.

The river water was the color of treacle, and the stones like amber. Lianas looped and hung from the tall trees along the waterway. Reflections dappled and mottled their trunks. And butterflies caught the light like fragments of blue glass from a cathedral window.

I thought only of what we had done and what there was still to do. Some of the young men, among them, no doubt, several ex-combatants, offered to thatch the roof. Others volunteered to carry mud bricks from the foot of the hill, where we had spread them out to dry, to the building site. Bala's wives would surface the floors with mud plaster and burnish them with dung. Bala promised to have some stools made, and a table for me, the teacher.

I spent the evenings in the half-finished classroom. It was now my place. I had strung a hammock under the eaves. As the day grew cooler I would watch the women walking up from the stream in single file with pails of water on their heads and I would greet the men returning from their farms. Then I would be alone. A kind of anti-Crusoe, salvaging nothing from his self's shipwreck, nursing no desire to recover the life he had led before and unfazed by the thought that he had no future.

At night I slept soundly and in the morning had no memory of my dreams. Was it because I was living in a dream? Lost to the world? For I performed my chores without thinking. Cooked my own food. Boiled my drinking water. Placed brick after brick on the slowly rising walls of the school. These tasks consumed me. I had no identity apart from them. I was what I did. As for my journal, it remained closed, collecting the red dust of the harmattan on its blue cover.

When I went out into the grasslands at dusk to sit among the rocks, the light seemed to emanate from the earth, and I thought of my parents, Harry, Ezekiel, Cosmega, not as persons but as spirits, diffused into the landscape and within me, but without form or feature, sharing the voice of the wind and of birds. As for Petra, I knew I loved her, but as an abstraction now, an idea. I was not in love with her; I was in love with the life that had once flowed through us. And it bestowed on me a calm I had never known before. I rested in the knowledge that it would always be there. I had only to walk out into the savanna at the close of day to be encompassed and reclaimed by it, at one with the rocks and the earth. Was this, I asked myself, how the villagers experienced the presence of their ancestors, the living dead?

The day we finished the school, I felt the need to acknowledge the event in some way. To give thanks.

"We must offer a sacrifice," Bala said, as he stood like a great stone in the middle of the barely furnished classroom. "We must consult a diviner and find out what we have to give."

I said I would leave that task to him and that evening made my way out of the village and climbed the hill. The tree was half-hidden in the long grass. It was an old lophira that had survived fire and thunderstorm. Below me the village was smudged by smoke from cooking fires. I could barely make out the structure I had worked so hard to build.

I sat among the stones, awaiting the right moment.

I let my eyes follow the gnarled tree trunk upward to where it forked. I imagined one branch to be my own life, the other to be Petra's. I saw that my branch had, at some time, been broken away from the fork, but had healed. I placed my hand on the mound of scar tissue. Under the rough bark I imagined I could feel the sap flowing in the tree. I felt myself a part of it, as if the sap and my blood were currents in the same stream. I then rubbed the black dust from the tree bark on my face before taking the bottle of palm wine I had brought with me and pouring a libation over the fork and bole of the tree.

Far overhead, vultures wheeled.

Around me the warm wind stirred in the grass and rattled the dry foliage.

## Morowa

That night I heard the drumming for the first time since the initiations. I lay awake, listening to the slurred and hurried syllables, at once lulled and troubled by the unflagging rhythm.

Was it my imagination, or was the drumming more urgent now? I pictured the Dununma dancers, stamping their bare feet, flailing their arms. During the initiations, Ezekiel and I had hidden with the women and children behind closed doors when the masked Dununma entered the village. We waited with bated breath. We heard its minatory grunts and cries. We shrank against the walls. It came like a dark and palpable force, penetrating the room. Frightened children hid their faces in their hands. Mantene clamped her hand over the mouth of her whimpering son. Then it moved away, its guttural voice like a river in the night, and the room filled with breathless chatter. The woman asked me had I heard it. Had I heard the voice of the Dununma, the forest djinn? I knew it was the voice of men. I knew it was all a ruse. But I had quailed and held my breath when it passed the house. I had shared their terror.

Tonight I was determined to meet it. Sinkari warned me not to go. I knew what she was thinking. She was thinking I did not have the stamina and understanding of a man.

The dancers had formed a circle at the edge of the village. Among them the Dununma, with its protuberant eyes, fat lips, and broken teeth. A beard of calabar beans and palm nuts hung from its chin. The bulbous face was caked with dried blood and the russet remains of chewed kola.

When the dancers saw me, they drew back. I could see they were looking for signs of terror in my face.

But I felt cheated. I had half-hoped that the stories I had been told contained a grain of truth. There would have been some mystery then, something out of the ordinary. But beneath the hideous mask was a mere man. Old Morowa. He stood abashed in the shadows, the ugly corkwood mask discarded at his feet, a clay pot resonator and pottery whistle in his hand.

A few days later, he was sharing with me the mysteries of the masks.

Yandi was a willing interpreter. Indeed, he was often so unobtrusive that I forgot he was there, patiently translating my questions and just as patiently translating the old medicine master's responses.

It was hard to guess Morowa's age. He was bent and frail, his hair grizzled, his few remaining teeth kola-stained, and he needed a stave to support him when he stood up. But when he spoke his face became animated as though the events and emotions he recalled in such detail had taken him back into a previous incarnation.

"When I was young, I was afraid of the appearance of things. The masks my elders wore. The stories they told of the bush and the djinn that lived there. I had yet to acquire the courage to confront my fears, so that I would no longer be in thrall to them. I had to become immune to fear. To see beneath the surfaces of things. So that life and death became one and the same to me. And I could see the world as it really was."

"What kind of things did you fear?"

"The djinn. Witches. The master of the Dununma. The dead. I feared them all. When I was small boy I did not dare venture outside on the day a person had died."

"But aren't the djinn real? And witches?"

"They are real. But the fear of them is in us. When you master that fear, you see them for what they really are. And then it is you who has power over them. That is what initiation is all about, isn't it Yandi? You get new understanding. You see things as they really are and not as you imagine them."

It is not easy, stringing together these snatches of poorly remembered conversations, to do justice to old Morowa's words. I wish now that I had recorded his story with greater care.

"I watched you as you worked," Morowa said. "Rebuilding the school. You and Yandi, and the others that helped you. I wondered what drove you to do this. And who you were doing it for."

"For Sangbamba, I hope. For kids like Yandi here, so that they will learn to read and write."

"And what will they read and write?"

"They will read about the world. They will learn about life in places far from here. Education will open up all kinds of doors to them. They will be able to help others and have a better life. Do you doubt this?"

"Everything is possible, but when you are old, as I am, you question many things."

"What of when you were young? Didn't you seek knowledge of the world? And haven't you used that knowledge to help people, to cure their illnesses, to protect them from witchcraft?"

I was thinking of the small boys who, even now, sought the protection of the old medicine master, sleeping on the floor of his house at night, asking his advice.

"It is true," Morowa said. "When I was a young man, I wanted to know everything! Even if I perished in the attempt! Even now, when the xylophones and flutes play the music of the Dununma and sing its songs, I long to dance." And he began chanting, in a quavering voice: *Sembe, sembe, sembe le, Dununma la, eh Dununma wo; n'de min i le nyonto ken yen . . .*

"It is hard to translate," Yandi said. "It means that the Dununma has great power. Its equal has never been seen.

"I remember the day my father died," Morowa said. "Up to that time my childhood had been sweet. I had been well cared for. I ate well. I was in my parents' hands. They loved me. I loved them. But then my father died. It was in the tenth farm season after my birth. Not long afterward my mother also died, and then my father's brother, Malfore. It was then, after these ones had passed from my mind, that I began to think seriously about becoming master of the Dununma. It was something out of the ordinary. As master of the Dununma, everyone fears you, while you fear no one. But the thing that finally decided me was the breakup of my first marriage. My wife ran off with another man. I sought to get her back. But this man taunted me. 'Show me that your iron can cut my iron,' he said. 'If you are a man, do what you will.' It was then that I took up the Dununma tether. You understand? Whoever sees the Dununma dies."

"Tether?" I queried.

"They tell women and children that a man pulls the bush spirit along by a rope, just as you lead a cow or goat," Yandi explained.

"So he killed his wife's lover?" I asked.

Yandi translated.

"He died," old Morowa said evasively. "My wife too. Her father a little later on. But I did not kill them. In the past, why yes, if someone aggrieved you, you would get up and go and cut off his head. But that time and our time are not one. The white men put an end to all that. That is why we use medicines. You see?"

"But what of the RUF?" I asked. "Didn't they do exactly what they wanted? Killing and burning everywhere they went?"

"It happened," Morowa said gravely. "But that time too has passed."

I went to Morowa's house every day now. Sometimes I just sat and whiled away the time with him. He would grate kola on a tobacco tin lid that he had pierced with a nail. I would boil water and make tea. But that was all. For I now knew that sociability may be consummated in silence.

Late one afternoon, just after sitting down with Yandi and old Morowa, we were approached by Morowa's two sons, Abdulai and Hassan. Both had made pilgrimages to Mecca during the war years and were, I quickly learned, averse to the idea of their father speaking of prohibited matters to a complete stranger.

"It is not good to talk of those things," they said. "We have told our father to put those things behind him and not to teach those things to our children."

Yandi tried to negotiate a compromise.

"Why not let the old man speak of what he *used* to do?"

The alhajis ignored Yandi and pressed their case. "Everyone here believes in the Qur'an now. All the medicine masters have thrown away their jujus. In our grandfathers' time everyone made use of them. In our fathers' time a few people embraced Islam. But now everyone has converted and turned away from those things."

"Yet without those things," Yandi said, "the tamaboros would not have driven the RUF from our villagers."

"The RUF destroyed our villages," said Abdulai, "because they were godless places."

As Yandi and the alhajis argued, old Morowa sat in his hammock, impassively chewing kola.

"Allah created the seven decks of the sky and the seven levels of the earth!" Hassan declared. "But he did not create jujus or magical medicines. Nor did Allah ordain that men offer sacrifices to such things or consult them about human destiny. There are no pillars holding up the decks of the sky. The words of Allah alone hold up the sky! It is the truth of the words of Allah and of his prophet Muhammed that sustains the sky and earth. You can build a house on a lie, but you cannot roof it or support its walls with a lie. That is why we must destroy jujus and magical medicines!"

I was beginning to think that the school, as much as my interest in old Morowa's past, had angered the alhajis, for Yandi had told me on more than occasion that they regarded me as a Christian, bent on competing for the hearts and minds of the young villagers.

"Have you heard how Allah built the two houses of heaven and hell?" Abdulai asked. "And do you know how a man enters heaven? The price of heaven is fasting, sacrifice, prayers, hospitality, truthfulness, and almsgiving. Consider, for instance, a child who loses its father at a tender age. You must pity the child and take care of it. You—"

"We do not need Islam to teach us this," Yandi said.

Alhaji Hassan, irked by this young upstart, picked up where his younger brother left off. "You must give to the needy. Whoever does this will go to heaven. And there are other good works: you go on a haj, you build a mosque, you sacrifice a cow to Allah, you undergo circumcision. All these things are the price of heaven."

Determined to show my solidarity with Yandi, I asked him to ask if I was destined to go to hell.

"Ah," expostulated the alhaji, clearly taken aback by the question, but loath to lose his momentum. "It will be an eternal imprisonment in ever-lasting solitude. Angels will torment and punish you with rods of iron. You will wear a gown of fire, and scalding water will melt your skin. There will be no respite from pain . . ."

He paused, while Yandi translated this grim picture for my edification.

"Do you believe this?" he asked.

"I do not know what to believe."

"Then do you not believe that when you die your life will leave your body?"

"Indeed."

"Where does it go, then?" Alhaji Hassan challenged.

"I have no idea."

"Do people not dream of their kinsmen who have died?"

"Yes."

"That shows that they exist somewhere! You cannot dream of things that don't exist."

I was getting tired of this. I fell silent, and let the alhajis ramble on until finally they too exhausted themselves or were feeling pangs of hunger. They departed with a flourish of their billowing djellabas, white shoes scuffing the dirt of the compound, leaving me strangely unsettled and depressed.

I did not want to complicate life for Morowa, for he had made it very clear that if he did not heed the injunctions of his sons they would cease to provide for him and refuse him a decent burial when he died. Nevertheless, the old man was adamant that my visits and our conversations continue, and so with Yandi's help we now broached, albeit with great caution, the uncanny world of sorcery, djinns, and dreams.

"Ezekiel told me you were a teacher," old Morowa said, as we sat together on his porch one morning.

"Not really," I said. "But I would like to become one."

"That is why you want to build a school here?"

"Yes."

"Just as the alhajis built the mosque?"

"Well—" I began, resisting the analogy.

"It is good to teach the things that help us live. Not the things that bring fear and death into this world. The things that bring life. Look at me! I have mastered all the medicines that cure people, the medicines that kill, and the medicines that protect. But I have never used my powers to do harm, only to protect and cure."

There was a long silence, while the old man grated kola and conveyed it to his mouth with a palsied hand. I had the impression that he was organizing his thoughts, and so Yandi and I waited.

"When I was a young man I apprenticed myself to a master of the Dununma who lived in Yamisa, in Guinea. I spent three good years with him, fetching and carrying, meeting his every demand in payment for his teaching. That is when I became immune to fear, immune to the things that threaten us in this world."

I failed to understand what old Morowa meant by immunization and asked Yandi to explain.

After a brief exchange, Yandi translated the old man's clarification for me.

"The immunization is the most important thing. You wash yourself thoroughly in the river. You go downstream and your teacher goes upstream. Then he changes into a snake.

"A real snake?" I asked.

There was some discussion between Yandi and old Morowa over whether the verb *ke felen* meant change or exchange.

"Aha!" Morowa said at last. "It comes like this!" With his forearm, he suggested the form of a snake, then, with his hand held at a right angle he mimicked the snake swimming upstream with its head out of the water.

"Then it wraps around you!" Morowa grasped his leg and held it fiercely. "When it wraps around you like this, you are afraid. But then your teacher comes back and says, 'Leave it,' and you look, and the snake has gone.

"After that he brings some leaves for the immunization proper. Then he finds a corpse, seven days dead. He severs its head. He puts the head and the leaves in a pit he has dug, and kindles a fire under them. You have to squat over the pit and be smoked.

"After that nothing can harm you, nothing can touch you. If someone assaults you, you'll easily overcome him. If flies settle on you, they'll die.

"Then the clothes," old Morowa added in a hoarse voice. "Your clothes have to be fumigated in the same way. Finally, I put on the clothes. I wear that sleeveless gown you saw me in the other night. If anyone hits me when I am wearing that gown . . ." (Morowa slapped his thigh) . . . "he will die. But if I do this back at him . . ." (another slap) . . . "it will nullify the effect and the person will live."

I thought fleetingly of what Ezekiel had said about allies and opposites, and asked: "Is the gown a kind of ally?"

"That is it! If the wearer is assaulted, *it* demands retaliation. And when the wearer hits back at his assailant, the gown is satisfied that action has been taken and it will not use its own power to retaliate."

"Could you prepare the immunization for anyone who wanted it?" I asked.

"Yes, if the cloth was provided. Even you, if you wanted, I could make you a gown that you could take with you when you go back to your own country."

"Could a person like me become master of the Dununma?"

"That is impossible. You could not take the medicines and masks to your own country. Besides, you are not used to the Dununma. If you saw it, you would shit your pants in fright!"

"But I saw it that night."

"You saw nothing. If you had seen me when I was a young man, you would have been terrified. The xylophonists and flautists would have been playing my music. Smoke would have been coiling and moving over my body. I would have lain on my belly and crawled like a snake. You would not have stood your ground. But I am old now. I cannot do it any more. I drew the Dununma tether for twenty-eight years. But now I have stopped. I cannot do it."

"It is not just because you are old," Yandi said. "It is because of your sons."

"You said that the medicines and masks were not real," I said. "I am not sure I understand this."

"The Dununma does not come from the bush. I am it. I myself dress up. If our eyes met when I was like that you would fall to the ground in fear. But I . . . I am immune to such fear. I have conquered fear. I see through the things that you are afraid of. I believe in myself. But know that I am part of something no one else can see or grasp. I see that life is a vine. Each one of us is a tendril, clinging to his own small branch of the tree. But it is the life of the vine that matters, the life of the tree, the life of the forest of which the tree is a part. You sever a piece of the vine, and another sprouts in its place. Death is the end for one; it does not spell the end of the lineage. Do you understand these things? Will you teach these things in your school?"

The alhajis took their complaint to the chief's court. The school I had built was an attempt to draw people away from Islam; it was too near the mosque; I had persuaded old Morowa against his better judgment to support me in my work; I was encouraging him to return to the use of jujus and sorcery, to lead people away from the shari'a. After several hours, sitting in the courthouse, understanding little of the palaver around me, I responded with relief to Morowa's weary request that I take him home. He had heard enough, he said. He was too old for this. The same people who were railing against his medicines had been the first to beg him for protection during the war, to save their skins, to safeguard their property.

I cupped my hand under his elbow as we began the slow walk back to his house. It was painful for him to move. He mumbled his words. Occasionally he glanced at me as if imploring me to read his mind. But he never complained, and when I asked if there was anything I could do for him, he grinned toothlessly and said he was not a child.

I helped him negotiate the crumbling step onto his porch and steady himself before collapsing into his hammock.

"Are you all right, uncle?"

"I am as strong as hunger."

"Mi na la," I said, "I will see you later."

At Bala's, I sat in my customary place at the end of the porch. I heard the stubborn thud of a pestle, the soft crunch of grain in a wooden mortar. Overwhelmed by lassitude and disenchantment, I saw myself as a pathetic version of Kurtz. The school was a dream as damaging in its ramifications as the alhajis' dogma or the self-serving beliefs that had led a bunch of American bible-bangers to take Mantene's daughter away from her and place her in the care of a unknown family. And falling across my thoughts like a shadow was an older order, visiting upon Africa its own obsessions, drawing lines on a map that cut indigenous polities atwain and invoking a morality whose Manichaean simplicity made Europe the sole arbiter of civilization and reduced Africa to a synonym for incorrigible savagery. It was then that I remembered, or seemed to remember, something that Petra once said about the human will. How it was our worst enemy because it blinded us not only to the will of others but to those aspects of life that were not shaped by will or consciousness at all.

Bala tried to get me interested in the small shop he had opened in the village. Among other things, he wanted to stock some Western medicines. Which ones should he buy? I told him that imported pharmaceuticals were prohibitively expensive, even on the black market, and dangerous to dispense. What was wrong with the local medicines he already stocked in such abundance—the cowrie shells, horns and red beans for sacrifice, the pangolin claws for impotence, the small leather whips for backache, the alum and ground tortoise shell for scabies?

"People want pills," Bala said. And he described the multicolored ampoules of penicillin that he had seen me dispensing to old Morowa.

What sickness were people trying to cure? What ambitions and broken dreams underlay their search for medicines and magic? Not long ago, the RUF laid waste to a thousand villages in its misguided and murderous campaigns to cleanse the Augean stables of a corrupt regime. Even now, young men went south, dreaming of diamonds, and slaved away with shovels, picks, and sieves in muddy waterholes that resembled the bomb-cratered paddy fields of Vietnam during the American war. Their bonanzas disappeared into the pockets of the men who owned the leases, loaned them their tools, and selected them from scores of others to do their dirty work. When they returned home with little to show for their pains, they spoke of these big men in tinted glasses, sitting behind the wheels of Mercedes cars, bawling orders and abuse. They said they were sick and tired of being pushed around and locked out. Others spoke of their desire for an education, as if this would magically open doors to them. Yet even as I listened to their wild ideas and bitter complaints I would be watching the kids racing excitedly through the village in tattered shorts, T-shirts, and bare feet, as if this place was paradise. Or remember the defiant composure on the faces of the women as they danced. Accepting their lot, yes, but never morosely, never resentfully, but with the knowledge that within these limits there was the possibility of joy. But then I would remind myself that I, too, not so long ago, had found myself at the mercy of the same dissatisfactions as these young men. The life I was leading like a punishment. Dreaming of some elsewhere, or someone else, that might turn my life around. If anyone had told me to count my blessings, to accept my lot, would I have thanked that person for reminding me that reality was a cage? So when Yandi plied me with interminable questions about England and America, what could I do but assure him that I would do everything in my power to see that he got out of Sangbamba, got a good education, and saw the wider world?

Every morning without fail I went to Morowa's house at first light, kindled a fire in his yard, and made him tea. The old man would sit with a blanket drawn over his bony shoulders, stretching out his hands toward the flames. I kept asking if there was anything he wanted, anything I could do. He was amused by my solicitousness. He saw through it. He knew I was the one who could not bear to sit in silence, who was in need of something to do.

Sometimes he had me take him to the chief's compound where we sat and listened to the business of the day. The refund of bridewealth following a divorce, entailing the interminable calculation of what had been given and what now must be returned. A villager who had encroached upon his neighbor's land. An older man complaining that his young wife had run away with her lover. Sometimes we would take the path that led from the village and sit together in the grove of kola trees where he once worked, adzing and carving masks. He would grate his kola on the rasped lid of his tobacco tin and chew it in silence.

One day, walking back to the village with Moroma and Yandi, I said that Sangbamba seemed to be a troubled place. After putting my question to the old man, Yandi explained to me that he had phrased it in a local idiom: "What is the headload that people are carrying and that we cannot see?"

Morowa answered with a set of adages of his own.

"Morgo te do ka ban." A person can never be fully understood. "N'de ma konto lon." I don't know the inside story. "N'de sa bu'ro." I don't know what's in the belly. "Yiri don, yi don, so don, fara don, yere don ka fisa nin be ye." It is better to know oneself than to know trees, water, horses, and stones.

When we reached his house, Morowa hitched the sleeve of his faded gown over his shoulder, and beckoned me to follow him inside. Yandi he dismissed with a single word.

Morowa's house had only been partially repaired since the war, and his bed and belongings were crammed into one small room. I stood in the doorway as he rummaged in the box beside his bed. On the floor were fragments of tortoise shell, a few broken porcupine quills, a handful of cowries, a couple of crumpled horns, a trace of mica in the rubble . . . all that remained, I thought, of the healing arts he had practiced for so many years.

When he turned back to me, he was holding a folded gown in his up-turned hands. The gown was dark blue, dyed with indigo, and had several small leather sachets sewn into the seams.

He gave it to me without a word, grinning from ear to ear as if we were involved in some kind of conspiracy.

"Ko baraka baraka," I said, blessing him for the gift.

I may as well have cursed him, for when I went to his house next morning I discovered him lying comatose on his bed, his blanket thrown aside, and a mug of water spilled on the clay floor.

When I knelt beside him, he whimpered a little, his eyes struggling to recognize me.

I ran to Yandi's house and roused him.

Bleary-eyed, he followed me along the dusty lanes.

When he saw the old man, his eyes started out of their sockets, as if he had seen a ghost.

I urged Yandi to ask Morowa if he was all right.

The old man responded by murmuring something I could not catch.

"What's he saying?"

"He often talks to himself like this. When we stay with him we hear him talking in his sleep. He talks to his father and his grandfathers. He talks to his teacher.

"Uncle," I said. "What is it?"

The old man gnawed at the air.

"I think he is dying," Yandi said, without emotion.

"Uncle," I said. My voice was trembling with urgency. "I am here."

With Yandi's help, I got my arm under his back and helped him sit up. "Bring water!" I said.

When I brought the cup of water to his lips, he sipped a little. Most spilled down his chin. He tried to bring his hand up to wipe it away. He was like a bundle of dried sticks. His flesh ashen and withered.

Again he murmured something I could not hear.

"He says he wants to die," Yandi said. "He says his time has come."

I waved the flies away from the old man's face. Wishing death away.

"Uncle?"

I bent over him, waiting for him to speak again, but there nothing now but the rapid, shallow panting of his breathing.

Yandi and I crouched side by side, keeping watch. Morowa's thin forearms were drawn up against his chest. Flies crawled in and out of nostrils.

"I think we should bathe him," I said.

"I will fetch water," Yandi said.

"You should get his sons," I said.

While Yandi went off into the mist, I stood in the half-light of the fetid room, the old man collapsed in upon himself, consumed by pain.

His breathing rose and fell. At times it was so shallow I thought he had passed away. And his eyes were staring now, as if the pain was something he could see.

"You have taught me so much," I said.

How could he possibly respond? Yet I spoke again, as Yandi appeared in the doorway, breathless, followed by the alhajis. "I have much to thank you for," I said.

"He can't hear you," Yandi said.

It made no difference. I had to speak. To defeat the silence that was settling around us, like clay.

The night comes on. The alhajis have gone to the mosque. I have decided I will keep vigil on Morowa's porch, having rigged my mosquito net above his hammock. It is well past midnight when I finally fall into a deep sleep.

I wake to the sound of children chanting their suras at the Qur'anic school. The air is damp and cold. I go into the house to check on Morowa. Nothing has changed. His breath rasps. He coughs weakly. His eyes are half open, but he seems unaware of my presence. I go out into the backyard and squat beside the fireplace, coaxing the coals back to life. I have never seen anyone die. I am not even sure that Morowa is dying. The word is too abstract, too unreal. How can one experience death? One can only experience life, its waxing and waning. One's life could be worse than death. And as unreal. If Hassan and Abdulai return, I will leave. Otherwise I will watch over him. I will have a pot of tea ready for him when he wakes.

I sit on a wooden stool beside his bed, with my mug of English tea. The now familiar sounds of the village reach my ears—a rooster crowing, grain pounded in a mortar, a child crying. Why is the world not slowing down in sympathy for this voice that is already silenced, this life that is ebbing away?

Suddenly, Morowa cries out weakly. His head moves slowly from side to side. Then his neck arches a little, and his broken, kola-stained teeth are bared in the frightful imitation of a smile. He seems to gasp for air, as if he were being strangled. Then it is over. His eyes settle. His mouth is agape. The room is utterly still. And I am quietly sobbing, as if my life has also ended with his.

I stretch out my hand toward the tethered ox, as the names of Morowa's ancestors are intoned. Yandi says: "The life of the ox will open the road between the living and *lakira*. His life will go to *lakira*."

Earlier, the praise singers sang his favorite songs, the songs of the Dununma. His sons' wives mimicked him, walking with a stick, grinning inanely, scrubbing kola on a tobacco tin . . .

Now the young men are seizing the ox. One holds its horns. Another arm-locks its jaw. Others grapple its hind legs. As the marabout saws at the carotid with a cutlass, red blood spurts onto the red earth.

At the graveside I help lower Morowa's body into the ground. His son's wives washed him within an hour of his death and shrouded him in white cotton and a raffia mat. Logs and stones are placed over the shrouded body, and the topsoil, followed by the clay, is spaded into the pit. How much better, I think, is fire and ash to slow decay in the ground.

We file back to the compound. The laterite is stained with blood from the butchered ox. Hunks of meat, black with flies, are being placed on banana leaves to be distributed. Yandi tells me that I will be given the heart.

On the ridge of Morowa's house, vultures are already settling. A sign, Yandi says, that the sacrifice has been accepted.

In the dusk I go back to the clearing. I sit in the shade of a mango tree and watch swallowtail butterflies dancing over the mounded earth. I know I will be censured for loitering here—giving false comfort to the unhappy spirit. But I have to know that Morowa will cross the black river without remorse, his worldy identity gladly discarded . . . a dilapidated house, an old rifle, a blunt adze, his habits of walking, his manner of speaking, his knowledge of medicine and sorcery, his broken masks.

# Night

That night, when I woke up shivering with cold, my first thought was that I had contracted the same disease that had felled old Morowa. As the darkness of the night seeped into my bones, I lay with my knees drawn up, hands clutching at my shoulders for warmth. From time to time I blinked against the seething darkness, fearing that I was going blind. Then I would make out the dim shape of an aluminum bucket, my journal on the table beside the bed, the faint beginnings of the new day through the barred window.

My belly was twisted and wrung with pain. I dragged myself from the house, out into the yard and behind the elephant grass screen. I squatted over the hole. The pain cut and seared through my abdomen. Nausea swept over me in waves . . .

I must have blacked out—for how long I did not know. I could taste blood. I must have bitten my tongue when I hit the ground. I lay beside the stinking hole, flies ascending and descending. I was shaking with fever.

All day and into the night, I drifted in and out of sleep. Often in my delirium I forgot where I was. Once I thought I heard thunder and the pattering of rain. I imagined it was spring in Cambridge. Crocuses along the backs. People walking along the towpaths or sitting outside the pubs in the weak sunlight. At other times I was haunted by grisly images. A severed head, eyeless, in a smoke-filled pit. A snake swimming through sluggish water. A morass. Entangled lianas. I was bogged down and could not move. And then the prognathous mask of the Dununma. I rolled over on my side in an effort to get comfortable. My bones creaked in their bag of skin.

People came to see me. They said little or nothing. Mantene brought food, though I could not eat. Bala offered me some pills. For a fleeting moment, I thought I saw old Morowa in the doorway. When Yandi appeared and asked what he should do, I mumbled something about weathering it. Whatever it was. It was only a matter of time before the fever passed. Just let me sleep.

The humidity of the day was worst. I would sink into lethargy, losing all sense of where I was, yielding to the bizarre rhythm that played over and over in my body and brain. The sweat pooled in my eye sockets. The blood coursed inside my head. And every afternoon thunder caromed in the distance and rain came pelting down, drumming on the tin roof, released like pent-up anger . . .

After five days the fever passed. Yandi and Mantene were visibly relieved. "You must eat," Mantene said. "You must get your strength back." But the very thought of rice and peanut gruel made me want to throw up. "Bring tea," I asked plaintively. "Some bananas if you have some."

Not an hour passed now that I did not ask myself: what shall I do? Have I reached the end of the road? Is it time to turn for home? Or will I come to rue this as a weakness, quitting now? I thought of consulting Pa Bockari and seeing what the stones foretold. But then I remembered old Morowa's words: it is better to know oneself than to know trees, water, horses, and stones.

I can recall little of my journey back to Freetown and of my first day in Pademba Road Prison. My weeks in Sangbamba were, as the saying goes, a distant memory, though I consoled myself that the police had not destroyed my journal when they ransacked my room looking for incriminating evidence.

I wake up shivering. The dankness seeps up through the concrete floor, through the weave of the raffia mat on which I lie. For a moment I falter between consciousness and oblivion. Then I make out the dim shape of the aluminum bucket, the faint lines of graffiti scratched on the wall—initials, dates of imprisonment, slogans in patois I already know by heart: *If you worry pass God go with you . . . All things nar God . . . Destiny . . .* Pathetic reductios of human thought, swathed and gagging in darkness.

I force myself to my feet. Is it any consolation to tell myself that twenty-four hours ago it was worse, far worse? That suffocating journey from the north, the CID interrogation . . .

"All we want from you is a statement of what happened. Alhaji Hassan has already given us his account. We just want to make sure that everything tallies. Then you can go free."

Free!

I remember the disdain I felt. The detective acting under duress. The junior police officers, in pressed blue uniforms, sprawled over their desks. I wrote down exactly what I thought had happened—the alhajis blaming me for old Morowa's death, accusing me of diamond smuggling, pretexts to have me removed from the village. It took two or three hours. I reflected on the irony. I had come to the country to retrace the steps of a nineteenth-century explorer, to see if any memory of his journey remained in the oral traditions of the north, and ended up concocting a narrative of my own to save my skin! My mind was befuddled from lack of sleep. In the untidy cubicle, a rusty Westinghouse air conditioner dripping water onto the floor, I had to struggle to convince myself that everything that had happened in Sangbamba was not a figment of my imagination.

"We have read your statement, Mr. Lannon. We've taken the liberty of correcting your English in places. You must be very tired. It must be hard to think straight."

I read the clumsily amended statement and refused to sign it.

"I'm sure you can appreciate our situation—"

"You keep saying we? Who's we?"

The detective took a different tack.

"You are in this country illegally."

"I have a visa. I told you my passport is in Sangbamba. It was probably stolen."

"I don't think you understand the gravity of your situation, Mr. Lannon. Do you know the penalties for entering this country illegally and for perjury?"

I was tired of the vicious circles. Why try to argue any more?

"You know why I do not have my passport with me. You know what happened in Sangbamba—"

"You had malaria. You imagined things."

"I remember exactly what happened. I've told you the truth."

I stand with my feet apart, facing the wall. I extend my arms above my head and place my palms against the concrete. It is the stance of someone being frisked. But no one has searched me. I have been all but ignored—assigned a cell to myself because, in the warder's words, "White men need their privacy." I thought he was being facetious until, on his second visit, he brought me an enamel plate of baked beans, poached eggs, and dry bread. "English food," he said and smiled ingratiatingly. Then he waited for me to eat. I refused to eat in front of him.

I change positions, stretching forward to touch my toes, moving through the barrier of pain, picking the locks of my body.

Life flows in me again. I shift my weight, adjusting my bare feet on the concrete floor. I am still sore from the punishing journey two nights ago. The heel of my hand is grazed. I wonder at the masochism that makes me lever my body forward, swivel my shoulders back, force my bruised ribs open. But it is *I* who impose the pain *in my terms, in my own time*. And so I undo the hurt that was done to me, that I suffered at the hands of the CID . . .

I sit cross-legged on the raffia mat. A feeble light trickles down the edge of the sheet of hammered tin that has been fitted over the cell window. Crystals of sunlight start from the nail holes, sending blue and white splinters into the gloom. Voices drift up like echoes from a world I have departed, that I might never see again. Voices out there or in my head? I do not know, or care. I am lucidly indifferent. I do not mind talking to myself, repeating unanswerable questions. After I refused to sign the fabricated statement at CID headquarters, what would CID have done? If I was going to be charged for being in the country illegally, when would this happen? And would my message to the British High Commission be delivered? And was I foolish not to have taken the opportunity that Momori the warder gave me—to send a message to someone I knew and trusted outside the walls. Cosmega? Ezekiel?

It is mid-morning when the bolts of the cell door are slammed back. A sudden rush of panic. I clamp a hand over my eyes, cringing from the light. Then I recognize the pug-ugly face of Momori.

Already I know the drill. I pick up my lavatory bucket and pad past him through the open door. Momori smells of soap. Perhaps it is his protection against the contaminating foulness of the prison.

We are one floor up. The air is hot and sticky, the iron catwalk warm against the soles of my feet. Momori's hobnails ring noisily behind me, echoing vacantly in the dung-spattered rafters.

Entering the washhouse, I hold my breath. The stench of piss and shit is nauseating. I turn my face away with revulsion as I empty my own shit down the hole in the concrete floor. Then I fill the bucket from a brass faucet and sluice the concrete around the hole. Flies swarm up.

As I strip to wash, Momori watches as if it's the first time he's seen a white man naked. I hesitate. He averts his eyes. I drag off my jeans and soiled underpants and stand under the shower. My skin is raw from heat rash, but the water is cool and soothing. I splash it over my face, neck, arms, and chest, wash around my crotch and anus, scrub at the grime between my toes. There is no soap—only a few smears of Lifebuoy on the concrete ledge—further evidence that I am taken to the washhouse only after all the other prisoners in the wing have finished their ablutions and been returned to their cells.

I have no towel. I step off the broken wooden pallet holding my hand over my testicles. Momori has gathered up my soiled jeans. The evidence of my humiliation. He nods toward the mauve-colored denim shirt and shorts on the bench beside him.

"You real prisoner now," he says, as though the prison garb will give me identity and dignity.

I accept the identification without qualms, even with relief. It allows me to ask him why I am kept apart from the other prisoners.

"You are English," Momori says, either in answer to my question or in response to my nakedness.

Another question forms in my mind, but I let it pass. I dress and plod back to my cell in the ill-fitting uniform, with Momori clumping along the iron catwalk ahead of me, arms hanging from the sleeves of his shirt like charred sticks.

It is a bad moment, reentering the darkness. Perhaps Momori senses this.

"Real African chop today!" he announces, and looks with relish at the plate of congealed rice and fish gruel that has been left on the threshold of the cell.

The bucket clatters as I set it down.

"I want to take that tin sheet away from the window," I tell him. "I need more light."

He looks apprehensive. He slowly surveys the cell with his bloodshot eyes, then cranes and twists his neck to examine the empty light socket in a battered wire cage above the door. He points at it with his baton.

"You want light?"

"Yes, and fresh air. I can hardly breath in here."

"There's only a wall outside the window. You want to look at a wall?"

"Can't you see the sky?"

"Why do you want to see the sky?"

I give up and shuffle away from the door, into the gloom.

Momori's eyes return to the light socket. Then he turns, and the door clangs shut. The bolt is slid home with unbearable finality. I hear the rattle of keys.

I shudder in the darkness. I do not want to be left alone. For a moment, I am a child, feeling how unfair it all is, how undeserved!

Slowly my eyes get accustomed to the gloom. I feel calmer. I persuade myself that the window is better left covered, that the tin sheet keeps mosquitoes out, that a light in the cell would be as beyond my control as the darkness.

The nights are worst. In the mornings there are things to do—the exercises that bring life back into my cramped limbs, the mid-morning excursion to the washhouse, the exchange of words with Momori, the meal, always the same now, of glutinous rice and fish gruel. I have made myself slow down. I walk around my cell with a measured pace. I prolong my time in the washhouse as much as Momori will allow. I perform my tasks with immense deliberation. I sit over my plate of food, chewing every fish bone, savoring every grain of rice.

In the brief intervals outside my cell, I am reminded of a world I have almost forgotten. A glimpse of blue sky through a barred transom window fills me elation and longing. The tip of a palm frond dipping in the breeze mesmerizes me. The sound of distant traffic, the blare of a car horn bring me to the verge of tears. Yesterday I thought I heard a woman laughing.

In the afternoon the heat lays me out. I sink into a drowsy torpor. My lips crack. My beard itches. My chafed skin burns.

When I wake, it takes me a long time to get my bearings, to free my consciousness from the morass of sleep. I watch the splintered diamonds of light in the sheet of tin over the window. I listen to the cockroaches scraping around the jagged edge of the tin. I lie in abject immobility, my mind in a fug. Then suddenly I am back in Sangbamba.

Night falls with a clangor of iron gates, the clatter of hobnails on the catwalk, prisoners shouting. My cell gets cooler. The spangles of light in the nail holes become dull and watery. I have got through another day.

But as soon as I lie down the panic begins. I fear the nightmares that lie before me, in which I am gagged and bound. I hear the cockroaches scuttling across the concrete. The darkness is a blanket or shroud about to settle over me. I leap to my feet and pace about, taking deep breaths, feeling my way around the walls. I lie down again. But this time the panic engulfs me like a wave. I fight for my sanity, fearing I will fragment and float away into the darkness. It is like tons of water above me, the darkness against which I struggle. I imagine returning to England. I imagine the spring, crocuses pushing up through the snow along the banks of the Cam, the sun on the cornices of King's Chapel, the great elm bursting into leaf. I walk along Trinity Street looking down at the worn flagstones. I remember every passageway, every shop. I saunter along Petty Cury. I sit in the cobbled yard of the Red Lion waiting for Petra. She walks in, arms enfolding a pile of library books, her scarf flung around her neck, a smile on her face.

Cambridge. The university library. She was always there, working at a carel on the third floor. She never glanced up when people walked along the stacks, brushing her elbow or books. There was something self-contained about her that intrigued, then obsessed, me. And she was beautiful. Irish, I thought, the dark hair, high cheekbones, wind-chafed skin. My face burned whenever I passed her. I could not bring myself to steal a glance at the books she was reading. The thought of approaching her, speaking to her, sent me into a panic. Yet I was desperately afraid that one day I would go up to the third floor and she would no longer be there. Term would be over. She would have gone down. I would never see her again.

I stood beside her. "I was wondering if you would you like to have a coffee with me?"

She didn't appear suspicious or annoyed. In the most matter-of-fact tone of voice she simply said, "I'm very busy right now."

"Perhaps some other time?"

"I'm sorry," she said, "I really am busy."

"When will you be free?"

She looked at me, her eyes as blue as the sea.

"I'm not good at metaphysics?" she said.

"And I'm obviously not doing a very good job of asking you out."

"Perhaps this afternoon," she said.

I spent the next few hours in a daze. There was no question of attending the seminar at Johns. I walked the streets. I browsed in Bowes and Bowes. I went back to my college room, but could not sit still. I went to the café half an hour before the time we had agreed to meet. It was crowded with Japanese men in blue blazers reading tourist brochures over Devonshire teas. My hands were moist. I started every time someone walked into the room. The book I had bought with me remained unopened on the table.

And then she was there, in the doorway, looking around.

I stood up and walked nervously toward her.

"Hello," she said.

"I'm glad you could make it."

"Have you already had coffee?"

"No, I was waiting for you. I didn't think you'd come."

"Do you *want* coffee?" she said.

"Of course," I said.

We waited to be served. I didn't know what to say to her. The wait was interminable.

And then we were sitting down together, and I couldn't get over the fact that she was actually there and that she was, unlike the person I had imagined, a complete stranger.

We introduced ourselves without shaking hands. We talked about our parents and where we had spent our childhoods. We compared the pleasures of walking on the downs (her country) with the pleasures of the moors (my stamping ground). We discovered a shared love of France. Petra had attended a lycée in Tours for a while after her parents separated. I spoke a little of Provence, where I had spent a summer cycling and camping. We agreed the coffee we were drinking was execrable. And she asked me what I was reading.

It was *Justine*.

"Are you reading English?" I asked.

"I'm in my final year of tripos," she said. She was in the throes of writing an essay on Joseph Conrad.

"With so many books written about Conrad," I said, "what is there left to say?"

"That depends," she said, "on your idea of criticism. If you think the critic's job is to read an author's mind, then there probably isn't much to add to what's already been written. But I think of a text as a refracting mirror, like the sea, in which you see fragments of the author's world as well as your own. I think the art of critical writing is to show how these different images overlap and chime."

"What personal experiences do your draw on when reading Conrad?"

She looked at me as though I had no right to ask. Then she said slowly: "Three years ago, I was seriously hurt in a motor car accident. I was eighteen. I was just about to go up to Cambridge. The whole world was at my feet. But suddenly I thought I was going to die. I lived my whole life in a single year. I went from youth to old age. When I recovered, I did not go back to my youth."

She scooped some coffee into her spoon, then poured it back into the cup. She appeared pleased that she had dodged my question and perplexed me. "So what do you do?"

"I'm thinking of writing my Ph.D. on Amos Tutuela."

She interlaced her fingers and placed her hands on her lap. "Why did you want to meet me?"

"I thought we might have something in common," I said.

"What gave you that idea?"

"Why are you so defensive?" I said. "Is it so strange that someone should be attracted to you and want to get to know you?"

"I'm not attractive."

"Perhaps you need some mirror other than the mirror of the sea to decide that."

"I'm sorry," she said. "I've really got to rush. I've got a class at four."

"Can I walk you there?"

"That's awfully kind of you, but I've got my cycle outside . . ."

She was putting on her coat, flinging her Newnham scarf around her neck.

"I'd like to see you again. Can I call you?"

She scribbled a phone number on a paper napkin. "Don't get too carried away," she said. "You'll only be disappointed."

I listen to the cockroach near my slop pail. Not far away, a cell door slams open and shut, and a deranged prisoner who cannot be silenced begins his mournful, nightlong cry in a language I do not know. I tell myself that if I can make it to morning I will be all right. I tug the blanket over my head, trying to shut out the demonic whining of a mosquito.

I doze off, but wake with the soles of my feet on fire. I sit up and scratch like a maniac at the mosquito bites. My feet swell. I choke back sobs of exasperation. I scramble to my feet and walk about, kicking my soles against the concrete floor in an effort to stop the fiery itching. I piss into my cupped hand and rub urine into my feet. It eases the itching a little. I lie down again, cursing the blanket that is too short to cover me from head to toe. I am feverish from lack of sleep. I am frightened of falling ill again.

She is coming toward me. Wearing a cream blouse, red sandals, and a skirt of Indian cotton. Her face breaks into a smile.

"I didn't expect you to meet me!"

I told her I'd borrowed cycles and packed a picnic lunch. "It's such a glorious day, I thought we might bike to Madingley or Coton . . ."

"Why not indeed!"

"Do you have to go back to Newnham first?"

"I don't *have* to go anywhere."

She cycles away from the station, moving ahead of me along the busy street. On Madingley Road she picks up speed and shouts back at me. The wind snatches her words away, and I pedal faster, trying to get within earshot. As she steadies her handlebars, rounding a corner, her dark hair, disheveled, blows across her face. Then she turns, laughing. "Come on!"

All my misgivings and reserve fall away. I fill my lungs. I want to cry out with joy and exultation.

As we approach Coton, she slows, and I draw alongside and ask what she is looking for.

It's a gate, she says, that leads to a track and an old oak.

When we find the gate, we throw our cycles down in the cow parsley and sorrel. I climb the gate after her, carrying the things I bought at Sainsbury's. She runs ahead along the track, waving her arms, turning about like a dancer, voicing her delight to be back from London.

She sits by the oak, legs folded under her. Draws her skirt over her knees as she gazes across the fields, making out familiar landmarks. Her eyes are narrowed against the light. She says the library looks like a prison.

"From which we have been liberated," I say.

"This is wonderful," she says. "You must have spent a fortune."

I spread out the gingham tablecloth and unpack the baguettes, the Kalamata olives, the endive salad, the Gruyère, the bottle of Pinot Grigio. "It's all right," I say, "my parents are wealthy."

"Liar!" she exclaims. "If they were wealthy they'd give you nothing."

"How was London?"

"Too much socializing," she says. "What about you? How was your week?"

"It was all right," I say. Who has thought of nothing but her and of her return.

I uncork the wine and pour her a glass that is instantly misted with condensation.

She takes it with both hands, then transfers it to one while she wipes the other on her skirt. I fill my own glass.

Then she says slowly, deliberately, "Tom, there is something I really ought to tell you."

Her face is pensive. She looks at me momentarily before dropping her eyes. I freeze. Everything goes dark. I have the impression of a cloud swallowing up the sun. She is already in a relationship with someone else.

"I'm not sure I'm the person you want me to be." She pauses. "Oh, God, this is so absurd. I mean . . . I don't want you to let yourself get too serious about me. I've loved the times we've spent together. I really have. But it could never go further than this."

I am lost for words. I nod toward the food spread out between us and invite her to eat, but she has no more interest or appetite than I.

"I've hurt you, haven't I?"

"You've surprised me."

"I want you to understand me. That's why I've opened my heart to you. I want you to know how I feel, how I've always felt about my life. I have always wanted to be strong. When I had my accident I realized that strength cannot be drawn from others or from things; it can only be found in oneself. I've always felt absolutely alone in the world. I've always felt that my life is in my own hands. All I've ever asked of other people is the freedom to be myself. The world is a wilderness. I want to go forth into it and be tried and not found wanting. I don't want to step back from the brink. I want to find the inner, not the outer, sanctity of this life. I want to find the heart of darkness, the nothingness that is something, and emerge from it humbled but not broken. I want to find the extent of my strength. I want to know myself and be at one with what I am. To accept adversity instead of shutting it out with the spiritual defenses I have at my disposal. I don't want to have any buttresses—house, marriage, family, friends, sex—unless my whole being is engaged in them. If I succumbed to these things, I'd lose everything I've ever struggled for, and my life would not be worth living."

"You must have suffered terribly."

"I don't think one ever comes into one's own except through suffering."

We pick at the bread and black olives, isolated in the landscape, stranded with our separate thoughts, unable to bring ourselves to remark the trivial, neutral things that might rescue us—the cloud coming over, the gorse in the hedgerows burgeoning, a lark climbing and plummeting in the wind. At last I suggest we take our cycles and follow the farm track onto the Coton bridle path back to Cambridge. She brightens at the idea. She suggests we have coffee.

We walk side by side, pushing our cycles over the rough ground. I feel I have nothing to lose. I say: "Do you think it's possible to love without possessiveness, without jealousy?"

"I think if we're faithful to life we cease to be possessive. I think we have to try to see our own individual lives in relation to life itself, as windows onto something greater that precedes and outlasts us. Then real love arises unbidden."

I glance at her, and her eyes are asking me to understand.

"You make it sound as though God alone gives life."

"Not God. Perhaps the sea."

"Does love always have to be so self-absorbed?"

"But, don't you see, it's just the opposite!"

We come to the stile. I hoist my bicycle over it and walk on. The hawthorn is in bud. Overhead, cumulus fleeces the great blue spaces of the sky.

When she catches up with me, I ask: "So real love precludes marriage . . . two people living together, having children?"

"I don't know, Tom."

And then I see that there are goose bumps on her bare arms, and she is gripping the handlebars to stop her hands from shaking.

"Are you cold?" I ask. "Let me give you my pullover."

"No, it's all right."

"Then what?"

"I don't know. I really don't know."

I am losing consciousness. Falling asleep perhaps. For a split second I feel that I am falling into a drift of snow, yielding to the cold, to oblivion. Then, like a shadow passing, my face is in the sun again and I can smell her body . . .

The day is windless and warm. Horse chestnuts bursting into leaf. On the river—a stippling of blue sky, white clouds, and willows.

She is reclining in the bow of the punt while I pole. Wearing the brass Kenyan necklace I gave her. Her eyes are closed. Her face lifted to the sun.

From time to time I allow the punt to glide into the bank, steadying it with the pole, so she can pick anemonies, primroses, and bluebells. We find an adder sunning itself in a clump of heather. We watch it for several minutes, wondering if it will move.

"Shall I give it a nudge?"

"No, Tom leave it be."

At Grantchester we sit in the meadow with the picnic lunch she has brought—"her turn," she said, "to provide." We hardly speak, yielding to the spring sunshine, made drowsy by the wine. The landscape lies under a smoky haze. Nesting rooks bicker in the pines, their high-pitched whistles punctuated by harsh clamoring calls.

We return to Cambridge in mid-afternoon. Petra takes the pole. Standing barefoot on the slippery stern platform of the punt, laughing at her awkwardness.

"I may not be a picture of elegance," she laughs, "but I *am* poling against the current."

"Like hell you are! The river's flowing with you. Look—you can see the direction it's moving."

We leave the punt at Mill Lane, and she cycles back to Newnham to change. We are to meet in an hour at the Market Square. She has decided it is high time I learned how to cook. Dining in Hall! *Dégueulasse!* Spending one's summers in Provence and not knowing the first thing about Provençal cuisine! *Impardonnable!*

I follow her among the market stalls, holding a Harrod's bag that she fills with capsicums, courgettes, aubergines, tomatoes, garlic, and red onions. She asks if I have any olive oil. Of course I don't. What about tomato paste . . . oregano . . . basil? Shall we buy fresh basil? I have to admit I have nothing at all in my room, apart from some coffee, tea, and Newcastle Brown Ale.

When she has finished buying what she needs for the ratatouille, she goes looking for flowers. She wants cornflowers, she says. They have to be cornflowers.

In the kitchenette she fills jam jars with water and arranges the cornflowers, while I uncork a bottle of Gigondas and pour two glasses.

She places the cornflowers on the windowsill. The summer light is fading. Her black hair is surrounded by an ashy halo. Sighing, she takes the glass I have poured for her. Her face is in shadow, her blue eyes as dark as coal. I cannot fathom what illusions, what intentions, lie behind her gaze. I look out the window into the quadrangle where dusk is falling. Beyond the high walls of Magdalene, the trees are smudged by a pollen haze.

We are standing side by side. When I put my glass down on the window-sill she puts hers down beside it. The wine is a dark ruby. I glance at her then, her face tense, a forced smile glimmering in the cloudy light. She stretches out her hand and gently touches her fingers to my lips. Seared, I draw back and look into her eyes. I am aware that she has chosen. Now I have to choose, but am afraid. I do not know if the love I feel for her can bear the burden it will have to bear. I have only to lift my arm, to stretch out my hand, but I cannot. I do not have the faith.

"I'm sorry," she murmurs, and makes to move away. But I reach for her, and allow the palm of my hand to rest against the side of her head. For a moment, she looks mystified. Then I bury my face in her hair and cradle the nape of her neck in my hand and press her to me, feeling her breasts against my ribs, her pelvis melting into mine . . .

It is morning. I can hear doors slamming, men shouting. The mat is un-bearably hard. I roll over, catching my breath as the pain shoots through me. The blanket is soaked in sweat. I am icy cold. In my delirium I keep forgetting where I am . . .

Momori and another warder have to half-carry me along the catwalk. We descend a helical iron staircase and cross an enclosed yard into a section of the prison I have not seen before. I am frightened of losing consciousness again. Iron gates are unlocked, swing open, clang shut. Knots of prisoners stare at me. We cross an open courtyard. The glaring whiteness of the sky blinds me. My eyes water. Then I am plunged into darkness again, down a long corridor.

The second warder walks on, and Momori guides me into a poky room. There is a hole in the wall. Above it a grubby piece of cardboard says STORES. Momori shouts "Lannon" into the hole. For a moment I do not even recognize my name. Nor at first can I identify the bundle of clothing and the pair of desert boots that are pushed toward me. Momori gestures for me to take them and put them on.

"Where are you taking me?"

Momori's face is grim, his mouth clamped shut. I strip off the mauve prison shirt and shorts and struggle into my own clothes. I transfer my scraps of paper from the pocket of my prison shirt to the pocket of my jeans. But when I hand Momori back his ballpoint pen, he refuses to take it.

"Put on your shoes."

The laces are missing; my feet slip easily into them. But it is excruciating to walk, and I hobble slowly back into the corridor.

The corridor is a wedge of light thrust into the darkness. I hug the wall, limping after Momori. The darkness closes in behind me, engulfing the labyrinth I am now leaving. For an awful moment I think that Petra is back there, that I have to go back and find her and lead her out . . .

But I do not look back. I can hear street sounds now. Voices. I am moving into the light of day.

## After Fieldwork

A couple of weeks after putting Tom Lannon on a plane to London, I brought my own research to an end and returned to America. I was glad to be home, though my days were filled with menial tasks—dealing with a daunting backlog of e-mails, meeting with my doctoral students, writing the liner notes for a CD of the hunter's praise songs I had recorded in Barawa, filing a report on the research I had done in Freetown. Yet, preoccupied though I was, I often found myself thinking of Tom Lannon and wondering whether he had repaired his relationship with his Cambridge supervisor and devised a plan for continuing his studies. Spring passed into summer before I got around to writing Lannon at his college address and asking if I could help in any way—using my Harvard status to vouch for him, playing a minor advisory role in any Sierra Leone–related project he might now embark on. I was also curious to know whether his relationship with the quasi-mythical Petra had survived what he once referred to as his *saison en enfer*, but felt that this was none of my business, and did not broach the matter.

Tom Lannon's response was a lengthy e-mail in which he described, in his inimitable style, the "dissociative fugue state" that accompanied his return to the UK, beginning from the moment he walked out of Gatwick Airport onto the railway platform to wait for the train to Victoria.

It was not just the cold, Lannon wrote. It was the lack of any communication or mutual awareness among the people with whom I mingled and among whom I now moved. I had never realized what strangers we are to one another in the crowded, cosmopolitan cities we celebrate as places of vitality and promise. As the train to Victoria slid and lumbered over the rails, people dozed, heads lolling against the seat wings, or looked out the windows, staring through their own reflections at a landscape smudged with green yet devoid of life. In London I walked the streets like a revenant, breathing the air of northern latitudes—the fug of diesel fumes and newspapers, chocolate and fried food. People scurried past, bent on business, faces deadpan, fretful, set against the wind. I passed the Lukács Beauty School, a hair boutique called Camus, the fashion houses of Adorno and Céline! The names no longer belonged to the individuals I associated them with. Generations had come and gone, and the original names had been forgotten. I had a strong sense that I did not belong, that I had never really lived there at all. And Sierra Leone was just as suddenly cut off from me, as though it had never existed. A record shop, open to the street, blasted out a new hit single. Several shrieking girls streamed past me. In Soho I found myself looking down a flight of stairs into a basement room. The walls of the stairwell were bright red, plastered with silver stars and black and white photos of strippers. A naked woman appeared at the foot of the stairs. I looked at her doughy flesh, the tinsel boa cascading from her hand, and she looked casually back at me like an animal disturbed at a waterhole.

At the London School of Hygiene and Tropical Medicine I submitted to various tests. Brights Disease was suspected. The discolored urine. The back pains and nausea. I was told to come back in a week and see a specialist.

I went up to Cambridge to see Petra. Unused to each other, neither of us knew what to say or do. I hesitated to offer her a drink, or say how radiant she looked. I didn't want her to misconstrue the gesture.

"I realize how difficult this must be," I said. "After all the hurt I have caused you. But I hoped we could talk."

"Talk? You mean like in an American movie? *Look, we have to talk.*"

We were in her room at Newnham. She asked me to sit down. When I did do, she continued standing and stared at me until I could no longer meet her gaze.

Realizing how hopeless my situation was, I confessed as casually and dismissively as possible, my brief affair with Cosmega.

She seemed unsurprised. Perhaps I had confirmed her worst suspicions, and she would now show me the door.

"You said you had some tests done," she said. "Did they test for—My God, look at me—I can't even finish the sentence."

"You mean AIDS?"

"All right then, AIDS."

"What can I say? I don't want to insult you with apologies."

"Let's not talk about it, then. After all, it's your business, your life.'"

"I remember you once telling me, not long after we met, that we cannot come into our own except through suffering, through submitting ourselves to pain. Can't you see that I might have submitted myself to the same baptism of fire you went through after your accident, that Sierra Leone has been my initiation—"

"And what movie, pray tell, did you get that line from?"

I did not know how to negotiate her cynicism and anger. I said: "We will have to get to know each other again in the light of how we have changed. I do not think we are strangers to each other, even though we are estranged."

"Knowledge isn't the issue, Tom. It's all about trust. A matter of what one can take for granted in a relationship." She paused. "And what about that African friend of yours, whose wife you slept with?"

"I've made my peace with them."

"*Sleep after toil, port after stormy seas, ease after war, death after life does greatly please.*"

"*The Faerie Queen.*"

"I was being ironic. It's not so easy. It's not like water under the bridge."

"Don't you see I'm looking for a bridge," I said.

Robed in a flimsy medical gown, waiting in a cold corridor, I remembered Petra's coldness and the depressing familiarity of Cambridge. I had not even contacted Harry. Other friends I had glimpsed in the distance, black gowns billowing. I imagined them complaining about assignments, casual affairs, rising tuition fees. I had died to this life. England seemed to have succumbed to an insidious global conspiracy that had reduced existence to a matter of careful planning, rational calculation, accountancy, and routine. A vast managerial enterprise, ruled by the profit motive, shored up against the contingencies of illness, spontaneity, and passion. In Sierra Leone existence was quotidian struggle. Long-term guarantees did not exist. One lived without protection, hard up against the waywardness of life, its concealed pitfalls, its corrosive enmities. You learned to take life one day at a time, never allowing oneself the luxury of self-satisfaction if things went smoothly or the indulgence of despair when misfortunes, obeying the proverbial prescription, did not come singly. I missed the ebullience with which people greeted old friends or distant kin, rapping for hours about everything and nothing! The value placed on conviviality, the sheer pleasure of the company of others . . .

It was not my illness that made me take stock, or my estrangement from Petra. It was the unshareability of my experience. I recalled what Ezekiel once said about the first rumors of rebel atrocities. One simply could not take them in. They were too far-fetched. And I thought of my father's stories of his father returning to Todmorden after the war. Taken prisoner in Greece, he and others had been by turns force-marched and trucked across Europe, ending up in Poland where they were put to work in a cement factory. He survived deprivations it would take him twenty years to speak about, coming home to find that his parents had planted hollyhocks and delphiniums outside his bedroom window in an attempt to make everything the same as it had been the day he went away in 1940. In four days in Todmorden he suffered more terribly than during his four tormented years in Poland—the trivial talk about the weather, the whereabouts and tribulations of family friends, the question as to what kind of work he might do—and the realization that nothing, absolutely nothing of his wartime suffering could be shared. He took work on a Scottish trawler and spent four years in silence and solitude, while my grandmother, consigned to her own purgatory, would struggle to understand the demons that gripped him, robbing him of the power to speak and act.

When Harry heard (from Petra I suppose) that I was back in England and unwell, he came to London to look me up. I asked him not to question me too closely about Sierra Leone. I could not deal with his habit of making light of anything he could not comprehend.

"Sylvia has not seen Petra for quite a while," Harry told me. "Like you, she seems to prefer her own company."

But Harry accepted my need for privacy and offered me the use of his pied-à-terre in Bloomsbury. "It's the least I can do," he said, "for someone who has come back from the dead."

Every morning, I walked from Harry's apartment to Soho Square and ate a leisurely breakfast in the spring sunshine. Sometimes I would arrive before the café was open and would have to wait for two young Africans to set out the wicker chairs and tables. As they worked slowly, talking to each other in a language I could not understand, I thought of Ezekiel working for a pittance at such mundane and thankless tasks, struggling to master a culture that he had neither been born to nor raised in.

My first visit to the British Library was as much a pilgrimage to the place where Ezekiel had undergone his extraordinary metamorphosis as it was an attempt to discover more about the region in which I had both lost and found my way. As I passed through the portals, I remembered how Ezekiel would copy new words or phrases onto file cards, then find ways of using them in his own writing. I asked myself what new language I had learned. Whether my weeks in Sangbamba been much more than a feverish dream. But I was beginning to write. Elaborating on remembered incidents, conversations—painstakingly piecing together an account of those dry season months in the wilderness. It was as though I had taken up where Ezekiel left off, finding in prose narrative the voice I had failed to find in academic work.

When Petra visited me in London, I mentioned my writing as a way of breaking the ice, of showing her that I had embarked on a new life. But, from the moment she refused my invitation to have lunch together, it was clear that she was interested in my medical condition, not my struggle for a vocation.

I explained that the tests had turned up no evidence of liver disease. But I had amoebic dysentery. And had had malaria.

"I must look a wreck," I said. "But you look great. Well enough for the both of us."

"Do I? Am I? I don't feel so great."

When Petra left abruptly, with the excuse that there were things she had to do, people to see, before she caught the evening train back to Cambridge, I was shattered. I had no right to detain her, to share my thoughts with her or ask her to share hers with me. I had bought a ticket in a lottery and would have to take my chances. The odds were against me, I knew. The habits that had defined our relationship had been broken. When we first met, the world had been ours for the asking. Now we stood in a hostile landscape of abandoned houses and devastated fields, all the props and properties of our old life damaged, scattered, and exposed like shards. I had assumed that it was the shadow of my affair with Cosmega that made Petra so bitter and uncompromising. But she had said no, this was not it. It is care we have lost, she said. We ceased to care.

I phoned her every few days. I asked nothing of her, but said I hoped we could meet again.

"Not yet," she said. "I am not ready. Perhaps I will never be ready. Only time will tell. It may even heal, though I doubt it. We have to take things slowly, Tom. One step at a time. Not just me. Both of us. Don't you agree?"

## Mistral

In Sierra Leone it had been the harmattan. Now it was the mistral. Blowing out of a clear sky, ransacking the trees in the yard, playing havoc with the dry leaves, roaring in the stone chimney at night like an express train. For days at a time we remained indoors. Over glasses of brandy after dinner, Harry regaled us with stories of frayed nerves and gruesome crimes, forgiven because of the wind. On Petra and me it wreaked a very different change. At La Boissière, the light flooded back into our lives. The dentelles of Mont Mirail were like a broken comb of ivory. In the courtyard of the *mas* the light seemed to issue out of the stones.

After a week together, Harry and Sylvia went off to see a Roman theater in Orange and motor around the countryside, visiting vineyards and Roman ruins. Alone at last, we moved our bed closer to the open window so we could see the stars.

Affected by the night wind on my face, I was thinking of Sangbamba.

Turning slightly, I found Petra gazing into my eyes. "What is it?" I asked.

"Nothing," she said.

I recalled our months in therapy. Having conversations we could not have had unaided. Finding our way back to each other . . .

"If you had not withdrawn from me, I would have done the same sooner or later. I know that now. One reaches a point in life where one does not like oneself very much. I did not like the person I had become any more than you did."

"If I withdrew from you, it was only because you mirrored so much of what I disliked in myself."

"What did you see in me?"

"It wasn't you. It wasn't any flaw in you. It was just that I saw the worst of myself in you. But it wasn't in you."

"We were too close. Even intimacy can be a kind of distance."

"I was possessed and afraid."

"Afraid of what?"

"Of not living. Of not being alive. Of not feeling as I feel now—with you."

"I have felt the same, many times. We all do."

"I wondered whether it was my academic life. The rage for order and abstraction. But then I asked myself: what attracted me to it in the first place, this need to take the world between the hands of the mind and wring it dry of meaning?"

"And then?"

"So many things. Always feeling the lesser person in our relationship. Asking myself what you saw in me. Walking in your shadow, always trying to make up lost ground."

"So that's why you always walked ahead of me, forcing the pace!"

I kissed her gently on the mouth.

Petra moved closer and pulled back her nightgown so that our flesh could touch. Our bodies seemed to merge without our will, a sensuous blurring and fusing that I had not experienced for a long time. Naked to the night air, covered by the moonlight, we moved as though we were afloat on the same warm sea, joined, conjoined, charged with happiness.

All night, drifting in and out of sleep, I remained aware of her. My body remembered her, the softness like a mist over our common landscape, the thought of her still alive in my loins. In Sangbamba, building the school, I had often been unable to sleep for the aching in my limbs, the soreness of muscles unused to hard labor. Now the same memory of the day returned, steeping my body, glowing on my skin, tingling along my spine. There was no one else in the world, no place else but where we were.

When Harry and Sylvia returned from Orange a few days later, we decided to walk to Gigondas for dinner. Our favorite restaurant was on the square, near St. Catherine's. "It'll be like old times," Sylvia said. To which Petra quickly responded, "Let's think of it as a new departure."

We sat in silence, inspecting the menu. I ordered the navarin of lamb. Petra said she would have the same. Sylvia said, "If I remember right, last time we came here I had the quails."

"And you quailed at the idea of eating baby birds," Harry said.

"Well, they could have made them look a little less birdlike! All pink-legged and pathetic—"

"How about the cassoulet?" Harry suggested.

"Too rich," Sylvia said.

I asked what everyone wanted to drink.

"I'm happy with the house red," Petra said.

"Harry? Sylvia?"

When the carafe of wine was placed on the table, Sylvia suggested a toast.

It was an invitation for Harry to do his Byron-Shelley thing and oblige everyone to tell a story—though we all knew Harry would go first, and in all likelihood no one else would follow.

But this evening it was different. Harry was in earnest. No hint of his usual levity.

"I liked what Petra said earlier—about the new. It's a paradox really—how far one has to travel before one sees what is before one's eyes. It reminds me of a Hasidic story. I think it's from Martin Buber. This rabbi from a Cracow ghetto dreams he should go to Prague where he will find a great treasure under the bridge that leads to the castle of the Bohemian kings. So he travels to Prague and waits by the bridge for many days. One night, after the

Christian captain of the guard has demanded that the rabbi explain why he is loitering on the bridge, the rabbi recounts his dream. The captain laughs, declaring that only a fool would believe such a dream, and he tells the rabbi how he too had a dream of hidden treasure, buried behind a stove, in the nondescript house of a Jewish rabbi called Eisik son of Yekel, in the Cracow ghetto. 'How ludicrous!' exclaimed the captain. 'Half the Jews in Cracow are called Eisik and the other half are called Yekel.' The rabbi, whose name, of course, *was* Eisik, said nothing, but returned home quickly and found the treasure behind his stove. So the real treasure is never far away, though the one who reveals it to us is a stranger, with beliefs foreign to our own, his world as remote from ours as ours is familiar to us."

"Her world," Sylvia corrected. "*Her* world."

Walking back to the *mas* after dinner, the dirt track was white in the moonlight, the vineyards steeped in the same pallor. In the ultramarine darkness, the furled forms of poplars stood stock still, as if the night had been poured like a poison into a row of stoppered vials. A sign on a gate read *Je monte la garde!* And there was a profile of an Alsatian dog.

The vineyards now vanished into the darkness, merged with the forested hills, and Petra and I fell behind until the chattering shapes of our friends had all but disappeared. The ghostlike dentelles. The balminess of the night. The scent of thyme and sage. I thought of the labor that had gone into building the drystone walls, terraces crumbling now beneath olives and holm oaks. All those lives vanished from the earth. The untold stories.

I placed my arm around Petra's shoulder so that we moved together, albeit awkwardly, along the stony track. Above us wheeled the stars, whorls and eddies in the blue fastness of the sky, such as Van Gogh painted during his final days at Arles. And I thought of those other nights in Sangbamba, of a blind storyteller holding his audience spellbound, the penumbra of a kerosene lamp, the fetor of bodies in a small room. I remembered the ping of a tin roof contracting in the coolness of the night and of how, no matter how placid the landscape, how cool our hearts, in noonday or darkness violence comes and cuts us down or, more insidiously, the pall of routine and habit settles over us until we can no longer breathe.

Insurrections: Critical Studies in Religion, Politics, and Culture

SLAVOJ ŽIŽEK, CLAYTON CROCKETT, CRESTON DAVIS,
JEFFREY W. ROBBINS, EDITORS

*After the Death of God*, John D. Caputo and Gianni Vattimo,
    edited by Jeffrey W. Robbins

*The Politics of Postsecular Religion: Mourning Secular Futures*,
    Ananda Abeysekara

*Nietzsche and Levinas: "After the Death of a Certain God,"*
    edited by Jill Stauffer and Bettina Bergo

*Strange Wonder: The Closure of Metaphysics and the Opening of Awe*,
    Mary-Jane Rubenstein

*Religion and the Specter of the West: Sikhism, India, Postcoloniality,
    and the Politics of Translation*, Arvind Mandair

*Plasticity at the Dusk of Writing: Dialectic, Destruction, Deconstruction*,
    Catherine Malabou

*Anatheism: Returning to God After God*, Richard Kearney

*Rage and Time: A Psychopolitical Investigation*, Peter Sloterdijk

*Radical Political Theology: Religion and Politics After Liberalism*,
    Clayton Crockett

*Radical Democracy and Political Theology*, Jeffrey W. Robbins

*Hegel and the Infinite: Religion, Politics, and Dialectic*,
    edited by Slavoj Žižek, Clayton Crockett, and Creston Davis

*What Does a Jew Want? On Binationalism and Other Specters*, Udi Aloni

*A Radical Philosophy of Saint Paul*, Stanislas Breton,
edited by Ward Blanton, translated by Joseph N. Ballan

*Hermeneutic Communism: From Heidegger to Marx*,
Gianni Vattimo and Santiago Zabala

*Deleuze Beyond Badiou: Ontology, Multiplicity, and Event*,
Clayton Crockett

*Self and Emotional Life: Philosophy, Psychoanalysis, and Neuroscience*,
Adrian Johnston and Catherine Malabou

*The Incident at Antioch: A Tragedy in Three Acts / L'Incident d'Antioche:
Tragédie en trois actes*, Alain Badiou, translated by Susan Spitzer

*Philosophical Temperaments: From Plato to Foucault*, Peter Sloterdijk

*To Carl Schmitt: Letters and Reflections*,
Jacob Taubes, translated by Keith Tribe

*Encountering Religion: Responsibility and Criticism After Secularism*,
Tyler Roberts

*Spinoza for Our Time: Politics and Postmodernity*,
Antonio Negri, translated by William McCuaig

*Factory of Strategy: Thirty-three Lessons on Lenin*,
Antonio Negri, translated by Arianna Bove

*Cut of the Real: Subjectivity in Poststructuralism Philosophy*,
Katerina Kolozova

*A Materialism for the Masses:
Saint Paul and the Philosophy of Undying Life*, Ward Blanton

*Our Broad Present: Time and Contemporary Culture*,
Hans Ulrich Gumbrecht

*Wrestling with the Angel: Experiments in Symbolic Life*, Tracy McNulty

*Cloud of the Impossible: Negative Theology and Planetary Entanglement*,
Catherine Keller